D1430749

BLACKTASTIC!

....

THE BLACKTASTICON 2018 ANTHOLOGY

EDITED BY MILTON J. DAVIS

MVmedia, LLC
Fayetteville, GA

Copyright © 2018 by MVmedia, LLC.

All rights reserved. No part of this publication may be reproduced, distributed or transmitted in any form or by any means, including photocopying, recording, or other electronic or mechanical methods, without the prior written permission of the publisher, except in the case of brief quotations embodied in critical reviews and certain other noncommercial uses permitted by copyright law. For permission requests, write to the publisher, addressed "Attention: Permissions Coordinator," at the address below.

MVmedia, LLC
PO Box 1465
Fayetteville, GA 30215
www.mvmediaatl.com

Publisher's Note: This is a work of fiction. Names, characters, places, and incidents are a product of the author's imagination. Locales and public names are sometimes used for atmospheric purposes. Any resemblance to actual people, living or dead, or to businesses, companies, events, institutions, or locales is completely coincidental.

Book Layout ©2017 BookDesignTemplates.com

Ordering Information:
Quantity sales. Special discounts are available on quantity purchases by corporations, associations, and others. For details, contact the "Special Sales Department" at the address above.

Blacktastic. -- 1st ed.
ISBN 978-0-9992789-3-2

Contents

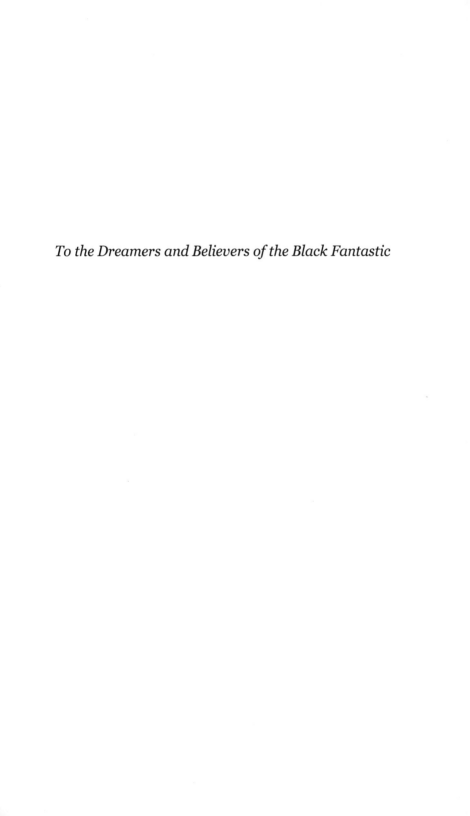

To the Dreamers and Believers of the Black Fantastic

"People have the right to call themselves whatever they like. That doesn't bother me. It's other people doing the calling that bothers me."
— **_Octavia E. Butler_**

TWICE, AT ONCE, SEPARATED

BY

LINDA D. ADDISON

"The shaman came together to find a cure for the sickness in the people's souls that caused children to be born sick. They changed into strong hekura—jaguar, ocelot, puma—and climbed the ladder of the earth to search for the soul-eater's path. The only way to save their children's souls was to leave the poisoned place, go beyond the sky layer. The people entered Ship to follow the path to the demon's birthplace, where they will once again change into strong hekura and destroy the demon's nest, releasing the captured souls so children can again be born strong and healthy."
Chant taught to every Yanomami shaman

The artificial sunlight of Ship drew sharp

shadows around the men sitting in the dirt of the central plaza of Bataasi-teri village. The scent of roasted plantains, from the communal fire, filled the air. Xotama stood in the shade of the circular village and listened to the wedding contract play out. Mayomi, her grandmother, sat within listening distance, nodding at their shaman, Hurewa, when an acceptable number of valuable items were mentioned. They were haggling about woven baskets. Hurewa, with his usual calm, simply shook his head at the numbers they proposed.

Mayomi had spent a long time, the night before, talking to Xotama about the planned marriage. No matter what she said, Xotama felt sick inside. A restless night made her feel no better today. Her life was haunted by a sense of being splintered. She had gone through the cleansing ceremony to remove the pain left by her mother's death, but no amount of meditation or rituals helped. Only her dreams gave her temporary comfort. Dreams of being with someone she didn't know, whose face she never saw.

"Tutewa will be a good husband," Rahimi, her best friend, said. "He's generous and not bad to look at. He's moving here to look after your grandmother, so we'll still see each other."

Xotama found his round face and deep brown eyes attractive. He had meticulously painted circles and bands of red ochre over his entire body.

She turned the slender white stick that pierced her nasal septum. "I know. It's not him, it's me. I'm not—" The expected path of her life caught in her throat.

Rahimi put her arm around Xotama's waist. "Is it the dreams again?" she whispered.

Xotama nodded. "I've tried to forget them but

she came to me again last night. I can't do this now." She pulled away from Rahimi and walked into the central plaza. The conversation stopped.

"What is this, does the bride need a closer look at her husband-to-be?" Tutewa's father said. "Stand up, son, let her see how strong you are. There will be no empty bellies in your hammock. We are good hunters." He prodded Tutewa.

He started to stand, but Xotama gestured for him to sit. "No, I'm sorry, this isn't..." Her voice faded under their stares.

Mayomi rushed over to her. "Forgive my granddaughter. She's not herself today."

"She seems very much herself today, grandmother," Hurewa said. "What are you trying to say, Xotama?"

"I'm sorry, but I'm not ready to agree to a marriage contract," Xotama said. She saw Rahimi put her hands over her mouth.

Everyone started shouting at once.

Above the villages and forest, beyond the sky created by technology, a meta-plasmic layer contained the neural web called Ship. A Watcher let her mind roam the forest quadrant of the hollowed out, terra-formed asteroid where Xotama stood. Their minds touched through the bio-implants all Yanomami had in their brains. The Watcher's real body was in slow stasis, growing old a hundred times slower than those who inhabited the forests. Her mind lived in the virtual world sustained by Ship.

Today she worked in navigation, in the form of a green-furred monkey with four arms. Long fingers moved quickly over a multi-colored ball of writhing vines, tapping any ends that snaked out. Each touch

generated a bright spark of light, making the end
flow back into the center of the vine ball. The echo
of dreams shared with Xotama sang back at her,
just as they haunted Xotama.

She drank in Xotama's turmoil, smoothed it
over her virtual face, breathing in the sharp, sweet
flavor of discontent. There was a corresponding
hunger in her, a breach. Though she knew more
than Xotama, the knowledge did little to feed the
unsettling emptiness.

...tell me, what troubles you... Ship asked, a gentle whisper in her mind.

Talking with Ship was like floating under water.
She surrendered to the smothering, reminding herself there was no body to suffocate, just a sensation
in the mind, to treat it like a dream and enter gently, as if falling asleep.

(I cannot find the words) she thought to it.

...what does it look like?...

She let the hunger take shape: a dark circle broken in two, one jagged piece disappears, the other
grows larger, one eye appears in the center, tears of
light slowly fall from the eye, the dark half becomes
a tattered sail, beating wildly in a firestorm that
consumes the light, the eye begins to close.

...enough... Ship said, dissolving the images.

In navigation, tendrils of vine whipped through
the air. She worked rapidly to get the vines back in
control. An otter with orange skin and three pairs of
arms swam into navigation. He licked her face,
transmitting his genetic designation, and began to
work over the vines.

...I have tasted your discomfort for a long time
but hoped you would settle it on your own... Ship
said. ...she cannot heal without you...you must find
a way or you will both be lost...

She thought the word 'home' and was in her virtual hammock, in the vast circular village that housed all the Watchers. A neighbor in the shape of a golden panther nudged her with his shoulder. His touch was like an early morning breeze. He asked, (why are you afraid?)

(I am broken and I don't know how to become whole) she said.

Mayomi grabbed Xotama's arm to pull her away. Hurewa stood and gently moved the grandmother aside. He cupped Xotama's face in his hands, stared hard into her eyes. After caressing the moon-shaped birthmark on her left cheek, he clapped his hands to get everyone's attention.

Xotama looked at Tutewa and felt a flutter of desire mixed with sadness.

"What is wrong with this girl?" Tutewa's father said, pointing at her. "Does she think my son is not good enough?"

"Let her be, father," Tutewa said. "I want to hear what she has to say."

Xotama fought back tears, wanting to give some explanation, but she didn't know where to start.

"Let me tell you about a dream I had last night," Hurewa said. "I saw Xotama's birthmark on the beak of a golden toucan surrounded by other birds, with bright red and blue feathers, perched on white rocks. They rose into the sky as one, leaving the golden bird on the ground. A hekura in the shape of a young leopard crept into the circle of rocks. Its eyes glowed red. I recognized it as my hekura and stood in front of the golden bird as the leopard leapt. I took it into my chest and saw the bird's true form through the leopard eyes. A young girl, staring at her shadow on the ground, drawn by bright moonlight. Her shadow lifted off the ground and stood next to her. The moon came closer until it was so bright I had to run into the forest.

"What do you see in your dreams, Xotama?"

She took a deep breath and said, "There is another in my dreams, someone I never see but can sense. She has shown me many things. Last night we flew high above a green forest, dotted sparsely with villages, brown circular pots, their edges stretched inward to a flickering center. I wasn't afraid because she was with me. I don't know who she is or what the dreams mean. When I wake I feel like half a person.

"I think only Ship can help me understand what these dreams mean."

A young man from Tutewa's village said, "Women are not allowed to talk to Ship."

"There are women Watchers," Xotama said. "There are stories of women shaman. I don't think Ship cares that I have a womb."

This started the yelling again. Hurewa had to bang two gourds to get everyone's attention. "We live inside Ship, not unlike a womb. Without Ship we would spill into the airless trail we follow, our souls eaten by the Soul Killer. I'm not going to judge for Ship. Which of you think you can?" No one said a word.

"When I woke this morning, the air was full of big and small magic," the shaman said. "Xotama must walk the path of the spirits before we have any more discussions of marriage. Important dreams have to be honored."

Tutewa walked over to Xotama and spit on the ground in front of her to signify the path was clear between them. "I accept that you need to settle this storm inside. I will wait twenty days for a message from you. If I hear nothing, I'll consider our marriage bond dissolved."

He walked away, followed by his father and the three other men from his village. They ducked out the narrow opening of the walled village, into the forest.

Part of her didn't want him to go. If only she could push this pain away and be happy in her life. She balled up her fists. What was wrong with her?

Hurewa took Xotama's hand and led her across the center court to a shaded area. Mayomi followed. The three of them sat on the ground. They sat out of earshot of everyone else. More people drifted into the village center. Men, women and children gathered on the far side of the center fire, keeping a cautious distance between themselves and Xotama.

"A path of fire waits in front of you before your journey ends," Hurewa said. "The end is the beginning. Enter the circle. I have seen this as a waking dream."

"The circle?" Xotama asked.

"You'll understand when the time comes. It will take all your courage to heal this breach. The flow of this day has been changed by your words and my dream messenger. It wouldn't be wise to stop now. Are you ready to begin?"

Xotama took a quick breath. She hadn't thought beyond the aching need to stop today's events. "I—I don't know. Will you come with me?"

"No. You must do this alone. It will be dangerous. Not everyone who seeks Ship returns."

"There must be another way," Mayomi pleaded. "I've taken care of her since her mother died giving birth. Her father entrusted me with her life when he moved to another village to marry. I fear her mother's spirit lingers nearby, pulling at her."

"Someone lingers near, but it's not her mother." The shaman stared hard at Mayomi.

Mayomi looked stricken, opened her mouth as if to speak, but put her fist over it instead.

"You will follow the river to the place where no one lives." Hurewa held Xotama's hands. "There, if Ship is agreeable, you may be returned to the shadow in your dreams. We will sit vigil for your return."

Tears fell from Mayomi's eyes, but she said nothing.

"Let's go," he said.

They stood and walked to the village's exit. No one approached them. Rahimi looked like she wanted to follow them but her mother was holding her arm.

"What about supplies?" Mayomi asked.

"Ship will give her what she needs," he said. "We should go from here alone, Mayomi."

"Remember that I love you," Mayomi whispered in Xotama's ear, hugging her tightly.

They walked to the river down a rarely used path. The thick, sweet scent of flowering vines lifted Xotama's soul; their red blossoms made her smile. The hõrema bird began its afternoon song: "were, were, were..." A little of her fear dissipated in the air of the forest. This could be just another day if not for the fact that she was leaving everyone she knew to search for an unknown person in a place she'd never been before.

A freshly carved canoe waited on the bank.

"This is my personal canoe. It will carry you to the next place," the shaman said. He mixed some earth with spit in his hands and smoothed the mixture over the bow of the canoe, working a spell of protection into the wood.

"Thank you for believing me," she said.

"There is strong magic in you. I wouldn't be a good shaman if I ignored it." He helped her into the canoe, handed her a paddle and pushed the canoe towards the center of the river.

She waved at him as the river carried her away. The current moved well enough that she only used the paddle to push away from rocks or fallen tree trunks. Light from the afternoon sky, and the water's rocking motion, made her sleepy. Her hand slipped over the edge of the canoe, trailing in the current.

Xotama dreamed she changed into an eel and slid into the river. The other was also there as an eel. They danced in the water, slithering around each other, over and under thick tree roots. There were no words between them, just a perfect dance. Their tails and heads wrapped together to make a wing shape that lifted into the sky as, below, the canoe filled with water.

Xotama woke to water flooding the canoe. She tried using her cupped hands to bail it out, but the canoe tipped over, dumping her into the foaming waves. Under water, a tangle of tree roots threatened to hold her down. She kicked up to the surface before she got too snarled in the roots and swam to the bank.

She sat on the muddy edge, catching her breath. Now what? The river had carried her away from known territory, and without a canoe she had no idea where to go next. The ground rose, not far from the river, to a hill dense with growth. Trapped between the water and the thick bush, she reasoned that, if this was as far as the canoe took her, the rest of her journey would have to be on foot. Xotama worked her way up the hill, away from the river's edge.

In the overgrown bush, little sunlight passed through the thick canopy. Scrub brush and thick vines, in shades of gray, covered the ground, making walking difficult. There was no sign anyone ever walked this way, not even an overgrown trail. Pushing through whatever vegetation yielded, she heard a rumble overhead, like a coming storm.

She tried not to think about the snakes and rodents living under the tangle of vines and rotting leaves. Twice, Xotama stopped to dig a thorn out of her foot. By the time she reached dry ground, she was limping, her body covered with bleeding scratches. Despite eating a couple of tangerine colored ediweshi on the way, she was dizzy from lack of food. The palm fruit took the edge off her thirst but left her hungry and weak. The rumbling above grew louder. Nausea twisted her stomach, but she pushed on until she found a small opening in a hillside. She picked up a stick in case snakes lived in the cave; it would be safer there than in the dark jungle if a storm broke.

Just as she squeezed into the cave, a palm tree crashed down at the entrance. Her scream was swallowed by the thunder of a summer storm. Unable to hold back the nausea, she vomited. Choking on bile, Xotama squeezed deeper into the cave. She listened for sounds of something alive besides her but could hear nothing over the roar of the storm.

Too weak to go on, she crouched with her back against a stone wall. She would die here. Alone, with no songs or rituals to take care of her decaying body, her spirit lost forever. She cried softly, curling into a ball.

What made her think Ship would talk to her, even let her enter its sacred space to answer her questions? What place did her small lost life have in Ship's larger existence; in the journey of the people? Drifting into unconsciousness, her last thought was that she had no one to blame except herself.

Xotama stood outside the cave. Wind and rain threw tree branches at her, ripping flesh from her body. She felt no pain. In a flash of lightning, she saw the cave opening was almost completely covered with debris. She looked down at her hands. Bone peeked through the raw flesh that remained. Under the roar of the storm, she heard her grandmother and the shaman chanting. The ground became very hot, blistering what little skin was left on her feet.

Without taking a single step, she moved down the hill, back to the river's edge. Standing at the spot where she had climbed out of the river, she looked across the white caps of the water and saw her canoe rise into the air. Shoro, dark-feathered birds with long tails, were lifting it. The chanting grew louder. It was a song of protection from the water demons.

Xotama looked down at her arms and legs. The burning had stopped, and her limbs transformed themselves into wings and claws, like the shoro. The lost feeling she had carried her whole life became a single stabbing pain inside her chest. A ring of fire blazed in the sky. Was this the circle in Hurewa's warning? Trembling, she rose on her new wings and flew towards the flames.

She skimmed through the center of the ring. Her feathers burned away. Xotama fell, not down but up, hurtling through a tunnel of colors, to land on a soft pile of leaves. When she opened her eyes, she was an infant being picked up by her grandmother, younger in years but with the same face. A woman, the mother she never knew, squatted against a large tree, grimacing in pain as blood ran down her thighs.

Mayomi lay Xotama carefully on the ground. An infant cried. Not her, Xotama realized, but another baby, coming out of their mother.

Twins.

Her mother collapsed as the placenta was delivered. Mayomi cut the umbilical cord and tried to revive Xotama's mother, but she was dead. Mayomi's cries mixed with the hungry newborns' wail.

Twins. Everything made sense now. The dreams, the feeling of being broken in two. Relief mixed with anger. Mayomi knew all along that Xotama was a twin, and never said anything. All the years of feeling lost explained in one word. Twins.

Their grandmother picked the babies up and ran crying into the forest. She stopped at an opening in a hill, laid both babies down to examine them. They were exactly the same, except for the sliver of a moon birthmark on Xotama's face. Mayomi touched the birthmark, kissed the other baby, picked up Xotama and rushed away from the cave.

Inexplicably, Xotama floated above her abandoned sister, helpless. An old man came out of the cave and picked up the baby. A Watcher, his skin was iridescent blue, like the sky at sunset, covered with the curling patterns every Yanomami knew as Ship's design. He carried her sister into the cave.

The cries faded. Xotama was on her knees, weeding in her grandmother's tobacco garden. A reflection of Xotama pulled weeds to her left. Xotama shrieked in joy and grabbed her sister, pulling them both to the ground.

"It's you! I can't believe I've found you." Xotama

held her sister's face in her hands. She kissed and hugged her tightly.

"Yes, my sister," she answered, embracing Xotama.

Xotama pulled away, looked around. "But how can we be here? Am I dead?"

"You are very much alive." Her twin smiled. "I wanted a familiar place for us to meet. You have happy memories of this garden."

"You can make a place out of memories?" Xotama asked.

"Anything imagined can take form here. Is there another place you would like to be?"

Xotama looked around. Everything seemed so real, she expected Mayomi to walk out of the forest edge. "This is fine. I didn't know Watchers could do this. I guess there's a lot I don't know about Ship and Watchers. Before this day I didn't know I had a sister. I—I thought I was losing my mind."

"I know. I haven't been doing well myself." She wiped Xotama's tears away. "Even though I knew you lived, I needed to touch you."

"But if we aren't really here, how can you touch me?"

She took Xotama's hand. "Doesn't this feel real? As real as any two bodies. More real than dreams."

"Except in my dreams I never saw your face. Didn't know you were my sister. I don't even know your name."

"I don't have a name like you do. Here we know each other by touch."

Xotama thought for a moment. "Can I call you Notama?"

She smiled. "I would like that."

"This is unbelievable. There's so much I don't understand," Xotama said.

"Do you trust me?" Notama asked.

Xotama looked into the copy of her face, without the birthmark, and nodded.

Notama reached up, her arm stretching until it touched the sky. Xotama looked down at where her sister held her hand. Their flesh melted together. Xotama's eyes closed. She felt as if she was falling asleep again.

They were a wind moving over forests, flowing up into the false sky of Ship, swiftly passing through a thick wall until they were beyond the asteroid's shell and in outer space. Points of light shimmered around them. Below, a long, dark sliver laid against the starry background: the rough rock that contained everyone Xotama loved, everything she knew of life. They plummeted down, through the vessel's strata of protective minerals, into its meta-plasmic web, caught like insects in the immense memory banks of the intelligence called Ship. It existed in the living plasma that flowed through the outer shell, and under the forest ground. It was more than a machine and less than human.

Images from Ship's memory rushed past: First Earth, twisted, dying infants born to sick mothers, poison in the air, in the ground, in many humans: DNA spirals mangled into broken, twisted puzzle pieces; another memory bank filled with an endless stream of undamaged genetic codes, tagged and indexed, the genes of the Yanomami living inside the rock as it hurtled through space. Each new marriage, each new infant produces another flow of genetic possibilities. Xotama and Notama's genetic history undulated from First Earth and extrapolated into patterns that exploded into data streams that even Notama had not experienced.

More and more information poured into their minds. They saw the debates that led to the decision to maintain the forest society among the villages; to keep the people safe and sane during a long journey that would see the birth and death of generations. They saw the bodies of Watchers in stasis pods, clustered like peas throughout the asteroid. Notama's body curled in a pod: still the size of a child. Older Watchers in gleaming blue body suits in the forests, observing the villages, taking samples from the water, ground, plants; surveying animals: wild pigs, tapir, giant anteaters; giant rodents, snakes, armadillos, tortoises, monkeys.

Xotama's mind was stripped down by the waves of information. Each new concept carried countless layers of explanation, information to explain data to explain information. Images slipped and slid into forms she couldn't comprehend. She wanted to tear her eyes out, rip her ears off, anything, anything to stop the roar, but she had no body. Notama was near her, also terrified by the flood of data.

They had unlocked something immense and it was consuming them.

(stopstopstopstop) Notama screamed in images: white lightning, bitter hot freezing decaying piercing gnawing...

Xotama was losing words, her thoughts tumbled into ragged sounds, tastes, colors...

green
pounding
sweet
red
wet
screech...

An old woman's face formed in the deluge of sensations, older than any Yanomami either of them had seen.

(Stop data retrieval, repair memory break, restore previous visualization), her voice was soothing.

The storm slowed and dissipated like morning mist. They were back in the garden of Notama's making, sitting on the ground. The pain and chaos faded rapidly.

"Who was that?" Xotama asked, gasping for air. She grabbed a handful of earth and centered on the feeling of the soil in her fist.

"One of the first Watchers. Someone who's been with Ship from the early days," Notama said, shaking her head.

They helped each other stand.

"I'm sorry, Xotama. I made a terrible mistake." Notama tears welled up in her eyes. "I thought if I showed you what this was, Ship, the world I live in, that maybe you could stay here. But I took us into the neural web too quickly, I almost –"

"No, don't apologize," Xotama interrupted. "I had the same hope when I found you. For us to be together. But I couldn't live with things shifting around me, or these strange words and things. I need to walk through the real forests every day on legs. I need to hold people. I saw your body, it's too young and your mind too grown to live in a world you couldn't fly in or change whenever you choose."

They held each other. "It's time you returned," Notama said. "I wouldn't want Grandmother to worry too long about you. What will you do with the information you have?"

"Keep it close to my heart," Xotama said. "I see that knowing too much, too soon, is not wisdom."

"Yes, my arrogance has shown me I have a lot to learn," Notama said.

"Will we dream together again?" Xotama asked.

"I believe we will, but without the confusion. Are you ready to go?"

"Yes. You are forever in my heart and my *genes.*" Xotama smiled at using the new word.

Notama kissed her forehead.

Xotama blinked. She stood in the mouth of a cave. Sunlight spilled over the forest. Other than some scratches, she was uninjured. This was not the cave she hid in from the storm. She had been returned to the cave her sister had been carried into as a newborn.

Her sister. Tears ran down her face and she laughed. She has a sister.

This cave was not far from her village. She took her time walking back, enjoying every familiar sound and scent along the way. She had seen many things with Notama. It would take a long time for her to understand even a small part of it. Maybe a lifetime.

For the first time, she looked forward to the future. She and Tutewa would marry, have children. Perhaps one of them would be a Watcher. Xotama wouldn't see the end of their journey, nor her children's children, but one day Yanomami would see the end of this path, and the beginning of something she could only taste at the back of her mind. Perhaps some of these Yanomami would carry her *genes.*

Xotama entered her village as the sky began to dim. The smell of roasted armadillo and plantains filled the air. Many people feasted around the center fire. Conversation stopped as she walked across the dusty space.

Rahimi ran up and grabbed her in a tight hug.

"I'm so happy you're safe."

Xotama pulled away, looking past Rahimi to her grandmother, who stood transfixed at the edge of her hammock.

"What's wrong?" her friend asked.

"Nothing. Everything's fine. I'm going to be okay." She hugged Rahimi back. "I have to talk to my grandmother."

She walked to Mayomi. Hurewa signs of protection were painted in red over Xotama's hammock. She smiled. When she left the village, the shaman knew more than anyone about Ship, but now she returned with so much more knowledge.

Mayomi met her gaze. Tears began to fall from her eyes. She sat on the ground in front of their private fire. Xotama sat next to her.

"You know?" Mayomi whispered.

"Yes, everything. I found her. She's not a dream, any more than I am. Why didn't you tell me?"

"It's hard enough making a place for one child without a mother. I had just lost a daughter, and held two babies in my arms. On First Earth, one of you would have been left in the forest to die. Here, I knew the Watchers would take care of the one I left behind. It was the only way both could have a life not filled with burden.

"I couldn't tell you what had happened." Mayomi looked down. "It's not permitted to speak of these things. Your mother's spirit might have been pulled back by my words, to haunt us."

Xotama shook her head. "You and I will not speak of this again." She took her grandmother's hand and kissed it. "I've found my lost self. I can be whole. Now we are both here." Xotama cupped her hands over her chest.

They stood and held each other. Xotama closed

her eyes and saw the rock, their world, hurtling through space towards an unknown future. She would marry and have children and, in spite of the taboos, teach them about their aunt and what she learned from Ship during that time of almost-madness.

MALAIKA DESCENDING
BY
SHEREE RENÉE THOMAS

I went to visit my Aunt Malaika, in Hell. The
bus took so long to get there, I started to give up,
tell them to let me off so I could go home. Seem like
we wasn't doing nothing but driving around in circles no way, and all I could think about was *Aunt
Malaika gone, Aunt Malaika gone.* She had died
about six weeks earlier, slipping on the wet pave-
ment on her back porch and breaking her hip. They
say she lay there, her wispy braids resting in her
white rose bush, the thorns pushing up in her eye,
until her half-blind neighbor, Miss B., looked over
the fence that separated their backyards and called
an ambulance.

Of course, they were late.

It took them two hours to come. *"Ain't no
hurry,"* somebody heard them say. *"The old heffa
already dead."* I guess there was no secret about
folk not liking my Aunt Laika. I can call her that
now, since she gone. She can't do nothing to me no
way—not with her being in Hell and all. Because if
she could, Aunt Malaika would have slapped the
taste from my mouth, would have had me reciting

Scriptures until I was hoarse and the black ran down my face.

Because everybody know that Aunt Ma-la-i-ka don't like nobody 'skimping on her God-given sylla-bles,' messing up her melodious name. You got to say four—*Ma-la-i-ka*—or don't say it at all.

Everybody know that—at least <u>most</u> everybody.

The last time somebody messed up and called my aunt, 'Miz Laika,' instead of her navel name, Ma-la-i-ka, she killed them. Actually, she let their daddy die, but that's killing all the same, now isn't it? That was one of the last times somebody had to call the ambulance to Alma Street, too, and it was poor Raybone who ended up knocking on the wrong neighbor's door.

His daddy, Mr. Wilder, lived two shotguns down from my Aunt Malaika's house, on the other side of the street, and apparently, Mr. Wilder had messed around and choked on a fish bone, sitting up on the back step by the kitchen. His son, Raymond "Ray-bone" Wilder, Jr., was staying with him again—he and his daddy had "an understanding," you see—and Raybone was so stressed out that he ran over to Aunt Malaika's house instead of calling Ms. B, or Ms. Perez, or anybody, like he knew he should.

I don't know why he did this. When I think about it, it don't make no sense. He knew Aunt Ma-laika never liked him. Whenever she'd see him, she'd screw up her face, jaws sagging, and say, "A 35-year-old man too grown to be sitting up in his daddy's house not working," but then she'd catch Mr. Wilder, Sr. huffing down the street again, his arms filled with a grease-stained paper bag full of whatever he'd scraped up from the church kitchen, and she'd just suck her teeth and stomp back into her dusty old house.

And even her house was hateful. The high porch steps sagged and sunk like they were ready to trip any fool crazy enough to want to walk up them. The back door didn't hardly stay shut if you closed it, and that front door would mangle any key in its lock. Most days she kept her door open. No need to lock it. Nobody was desperate enough to steal from Aunt Malaika.

Later, when they asked Raybone why he didn't just call 911 from his own home, he said his daddy's phone had got cut off. I don't know about all that. First of all, by the time the ambulance came to North Memphis, he probably would've been dead anyway, and second, of all the souls on the street, Aunt Malaika would have been the *last last* one I would have tried to borrow anything from. So I don't know what Raybone was thinking, but I do know, that when he woke Aunt Malaika up, beating on the door like he crazy, she cussed him out thinking he was the po po, and then charged him twenty-five cents for the phone call. If I'm lyin', I'm dying. Said that Raybone was as shiftless as his daddy, "didn't never work but always sitting somewhere, eating." Said his daddy was too big and greasy to be eating all that chicken and fried fish, anyway. And when Raybone said, "But Ms. Laika, if you don't let me make this call, he gon' be dead . . . ." Aunt Malaika started stuttering and sputtering so, that she snatched back the phone and slammed the door in poor Raybone's face.

Poor thang.

The ambulance came on by when Mr. Wilder died—about twenty minutes after they got the call . . . and that was a good ten minutes after Aunt Malaika turned Raybone away. Raybone had sprained his ankle running down her evil porch steps—his big old size fifteens fell right through the floor—and he had to limp down past old Newborn's empty lot on to Mr. Denton's place to make the call. But when Aunt Malaika hit that floor on 875 Alma, on the hottest day in July, she might as well have been laying dead in the street, because by the time that ambulance come, Aunt Malaika was long gone.

#

Reverend Preacher say in his sermon that Mrs. Malaika Hamilton had been a fine, upstanding woman, steadfast in the Church and didn't nobody sitting on those hard mourner's pews dare say nary a contrary word.

Aunt Malaika never missed a meeting of the usher board, and her white gloves and uniform were always pristine (a fine feat, given the dust she let accumulate in the house she'd been living). Aunt Malaika had been a member of the Church, longer than even the oldest deacon, and she had the dirt on damn near everyone. Still, she never would tell a soul, or at least, I don't think she would. Not many saint points in that. To Aunt Malaika, gossip was a sin. Even so, that didn't stop her from staring you down with that old knowing look in her eye that let you know, that she know that you know that she could tell if she wanted to tell and you know if you keep on backsliding, you know someday she would.

So when Reverend Preacher peered under his glasses, meeting the gaze of every one of us, we didn't do nothing but listen. "Mrs. Hamilton," Reverend Preacher say, revving up. "I said, Mrs. Ma-la-i-ka Hamilton. . ."

"Yes," we replied in unison.

"You know you had to get it right," Reverend Preacher say, laughing. "Sister Hamilton didn't tolerate you de-se-crat-ing her name. Sister Hamilton was a fine example to you younger folk on how to live in the fullness of the Word."

"Yes."

"I say, _the fullness._"

"Yes, Lord."

"And Mrs. Hamilton was born and raised in the _Church_," he said, clutching his bible, "part of that noble congregation called _Old School_," we raised our heads and said, "Amen," praying he would soon hush up as the ushers scurried in their white padded shoes.

The doors of the church were open, but who would have thought that Aunt Malaika's soul didn't float through them.

It was true that Aunt Malaika's 'steadfastness' had made her a hard soul to live with. At one point or another, everybody in the church had had some narrow dealing with her. Still, I was a little hurt, though not exactly surprised when I got her call. Whatever happened, I never expected to see Aunt Malaika in Hell.

#

I don't know what I was expecting, but Hell is really small. I can hardly get my hips up in here. Despite all the fire and brimstone—you know how they say we like the heat—you can tell that Hell wasn't made for no black folk. The hallways are too narrow, and the ceiling is much too low. It keeps pressing down every time you take a step. I nearly cracked my skull trying to make my way to Aunt Malaika's raggedy room.

And the woman at the front desk just as mean and nasty—had the nerve to cut her eyes at me, like I was going to steal something.

I walked down the hall, the sulphur so thick, I knew I'd be smelling it in my sleep.

Aunt Malaika shares a room with two other old women. I know this must be Hell because Aunt Malaika didn't like to share much of anything without making you feel guilty about it.

But if anyone could make a soul feel more weary in Hell, that would be Aunt Malaika. When I come in, she's sitting up on the top bunk, her fingers knotted and working in her lap, staring out a dingy window that somebody tried to cheer up with a yellow, faded crazy quilt. The stitches are all ragged and crooked, like somebody blind and shook-with-seizures sewed them. I can hardly see the pattern. I want to clear my throat, say hello, but it seems like I still can't speak in that woman's presence.

"Laika, baby, look like you got you some company." The woman turns to me, her piercing grey eyes look as if she could see all up in my heart and soul. I smile and turn my head away real fast, no telling what she might see.

Another woman clutching a photo, turns to stare at me. She wraps a tattered, navy blue sweater around her thin shoulders and smiles. Her teeth are blue and stained. She smiles up at me kindly, as if she don't know it.

"Who is it, Gladys? Can't be nobody I want to see," Aunt Malaika says. "Jim-bo? Karen? Hollis?"

"No, it's me, Aunt Malaika." I nearly choke on the words, voice so quiet, she can hardly hear me. I see her turn from the window and squint.

"Who the hell is 'me'?" she asks, squinting. "Ah, don't say nothing," she says before I can answer, recognition widening her eyes. "Got to be mealy-mouthed Mildred. You the only one that bother to keep my name straight."

I nearly fall back with the force of these words. *The only one...?* Damn. All that struggle for nothing.

"What you bring me, girl, 'cause the food up in here ain't fit to feed a snake."

I hold out my palms, sweating.

She looks disgusted.

I could have kicked my own butt for coming empty-handed, but hell, what a body supposed to bring to a woman that swear she don't need anything? I'd been trying to figure out how to please this woman since before I was born, and from the frown on her face, I guess she was going to keep me trying now that she done worried herself straight into Hell.

She brushed back her braids with the back of her hand and pulled a yellow cardigan over her ample breasts.

"Don't mind this," she said when she caught me staring. She tugged the *I'm Retired, What's Your Excuse?* T-shirt self-consciously. The long-sleeved shirt was a size too small and kept sitting up on her belly. "It's too hot to be walking round here in all that mess. I don't know what made your Cousin Hollis dress me in that awful, gaudy red dress. Knowing full well I wouldn't be caught out in no hussy slip like that."

"It was pink, not red," I said, "and I thought you looked nice, Aunt Lai . . . Malaika." Better than what she was wearing now.

"You *would,*" she said, narrowing her eyes at my flouncy sundress.

I was never her favorite niece.

She leaned forward, grabbing my wrist, and hissed in my ear.

"What you say, Aunt Malaika?" I could barely understand her. Her breath smelled like Juicy Fruit and minty fresh toothpaste.

"I _said_, don't you eat nothing up in here," she whispered loudly. "Don't eat a crumb or a cracker, and watch out for that heffa at the front desk. She sneaky. She'll mess around and have you singing a blues for every season."

"Okay, Aunt Malaika," I said slowly, like I understood. This heat and sulphur must have fried up her poor brain.

"You best to listen to your Grandmama," Gladys says. She was sitting in one of those green plastic deck chairs, her flowery duster spread out across her thick thighs. She'd been staring at a muted TV screen that was mounted in a corner of the wall. A skein of orange tangled yarn rested in her lap. I watched her pale grey eyes return to the black and white stories on the tube. The other one sat beside a faded chiffarobe, the vanity table cluttered with warped and peeling photos of children, smiling and gap-toothed. They stared back at me, making me think of ice cream and pulpy lemonade, the kind the other 'wayward' kids used to get when I was sweating in Sunday school.

"That your grandbaby?" she asked.

"I told you she ain't," Aunt Malaika barked, gritting her teeth. "I ain't never had no children and ain't never wished I could."

I clasped my hand, nails biting into the palm flesh. Before I came, I said I was going to be nice to Aunt Malaika, like I always have, but she was testing me. Though nobody could ever say I wasn't grateful for how she took me in and raised me like her own, I never much cared for the way she had of not claiming me. No, I wasn't her natural born, but she was the closest thing to a mama I'd ever known. And if I wasn't her daughter, I might as well be, because all the other kids, _Cousin Hollis_ included, was scared of her and wouldn't have nothing to do with her.

That's probably why Hollis buried her in that red dress.

I decided to change the subject.

"So how you settling in, Aunt Malaika?"

She looked at me like I had lost my mind. "Well what you think?" she asked. "One minute I'm minding my business, watering my rose bush—you know how they get during the summer—and the next, I'm trying to raise my head to meet My Maker. I look up and find myself in this Hell Hole, and ain't a real rose bush the first or a drop of air conditioning."

I look at her in disbelief.

"That's why I ain't never wanted no public assistance," she continued. "They'll welfare you right out of a good house and into the state penitentiary. Mark my words. Soon they gon' be roundin' up Negroes left and right just cuz they hard up and hungry. Gon' make it illegal to even have yo' own garden so you can feed yourself." She fanned herself. "But let me stop. You see what they got me in." She shook her head. "It's too hot up in here. I been trying to tell that old battle axe up at the front desk, but she don't listen. Talking 'bout 'take it to Jesus . . .'"

"I'm so sorry," I say, a little breathless. I'm starting to see what she means. I can hardly breathe myself, and I feel my sundress clinging to me, hot and sticky against my skin. "Why don't I open this window for you," I say, pulling back the curtain.

"It's _stuck_," she says, rolling her eyes.

No, she never liked me, but I was the only one who bothered to see about her. But I couldn't help myself. I wanted to fight it off, but here I was again, trying to prove my worthiness. I tugged harder on the window pane, trying to force it up with the tips of my fingers. It didn't budge, but I did see a sight that made me still and queasy.

The window was nailed shut, big red rusting nails driven deep into the window sill. But just beyond it was a rose bush, so big and beautiful, perfectly rounded with its soft petals and luscious leaves gleaming like God's Great Own, like something straight out of Eden.

No wonder Aunt Malaika stayed glued to that window.

That's when I started wondering what Old Grey Eyes was missing in that TV she was watching so hard, and Miss Thin—what kind of a sad story was hidden behind those children's gap-toothed smiles and eyes?

I keep staring at the rose bush until it moves. I think it moves, or maybe that was just——

A thorny branch snakes up and hisses at me, then slams hard into the window pane, cracking the glass. An odor so foul and thick begins to fill the room that Miss Thin begins to wail.

"Baby, just shut it," Aunt Malaika says, waving at the curtains. "Shut it quick before I have to listen to Velma all day." Her voice is tired, almost resigned. I have never heard Aunt Laika sound this way.

I yank back the tattered curtains, listening for the next assault, but the rose bush soon tires and slinks back into itself. The room is quiet, silence falls around us like a heavy shawl. Below the ragged calm of Miss Thin's breathing, I hear the low voiced hum of distant climate control. Perhaps a heater.

Miss Thin slumps in her vanity chair, the pictures tumbling over in their gilded frames. Grey Eyes falls back into the rhythm of her voiceless stars, their movements a slow pantomime against the colorless screen.

I sit next to Aunt Malaika, my knee pressed against her thigh, and stare at the hidden window. Aunt Malaika loved her rose bush. She prized its roots more than any sour fruit on her swaybacked peach trees. Before the sun rose, she was out with her rusty watering can in hand. And three times each day, before it set, she would water it again, sprinkling it from her cupped hands, as if it was her own back porch baptism.

When I was a child, I used to watch her from my bedroom window. These quiet times, when day-clean was just bending into daydone, she chose to be alone. She never let me help her, afraid that I might pour too much or crush the delicate petals and leaves with my eager hands. But she let me watch, and for that I was grateful. Her rose bush was the only thing of beauty she allowed in her yard.

"Remember how you used to wipe my eyes with rose petals, after you bathed me and put me to bed?" I say suddenly. "Your rose bush had a special scent. I ain't smelled it in years, but look like I woke up the other day and heard you call my name."

"How you remember a thing like that?" she says.

She gives me another look, not so long, not so knowing, then scratches her scalp, flicking dandruff from a white braid. I imagine the young girl in her, what she must have looked like when she was close to my age. She never had any pictures nowhere in the house, and anytime I asked her about her youth, she would just look off and suck her teeth. She still has that head of hair all the other usher mothers envied, and she still has her ways. I look around. I don't see any mirrors. I guess you don't need none in Hell. I wonder if she knows.

"When I was a youngun, not such a slip as you, but young enough," she begins, "them old mothers used to say a night bath in rosewater kept a girl's future soft and sweet. Something 'bout sealing a woman's ways."

I laugh. "That *is* sweet."

She grunts. "Oh, that ain't nothing but some hoodoo mess, them old ways from folk that don't know no better. You feeling mighty 'soft and sweet' now?"

I *was,* I want to say, *'til you got ugly*.

"That your grandbaby?" Miss Thin asks again. It's like her mind is one of those old phonographs, and she's stuck on the same groove. She's fondling her framed pictures, smiling, spittle hanging from her lip. Aunt Malaika frowns and shifts on the bed. "No, Velma, that's my daughter. How old you think I is, anyway?"

I don't say nothing, just look at Aunt Malaika.

"Well, what her name? You been sitting over there whispering and ain't introduced nobody."

"Her name Hollis . . ."

"—Mildred," I mutter.

"Mildred," she continues, not missing a beat, "has come to visit me, and we was talking, *minding our business,*" she adds with emphasis. It occurs to me that Aunt Malaika is possessive of a visitor, even me. This is gratifying, and I can hardly contain my smile.

"Well, Mildred, welcome to Hell, child," Miss Thin says, brightly. "I know it ain't what you thought it was, but we gone do our best to make you enjoy your stay. You must have done something mighty bad, though, something sinful to come down here, but I can't tell what it is, sweet as you seem to be. But you never know...they don't tell you nothing. Just sign you in and lock you up."

"Never know?" Grey Eyes snapped to attention, her head pivoting away from the TV screen. "What you mean 'you never know?' What somebody got to tell you 'bout yourself that you don't already know? You here the same reason why we all here."

"And what's that?" Miss Thin say, her eyes darting round the room.

"'Cuz you triflin'. You was triflin' when you was living and now you triflin' in death."

"I _ain't_ triflin'!" Miss Thin yell, banging her tiny fists on her gilded keepsake chest. "Is it wrong to want a little bit of loving for yourself? Is it wrong to want somebody just for you?"

"That's the problem. He wasn't for you. He was _married_, and all them children you doting on, sitting on that desk, ain't got no part of you in them. They his—his alone." She paused, doubled back. "Naw, that ain't right. They his—_and his wife's_."

"It ain't true," Miss Thin says, her eyes pleading with me. I knot the hem of my dress, fingers working, nervous—same thing I did when I was child. I don't want to hear this. In fact, I want to go.

"And if you had the backbone enough to love a married man, you should have had backbone enough to love your ownself!"

"Listen, I ain't the one who made them vows. When we met, I didn't know nothing about them! Why ain't you fussing at him?"

Grey Eyes looked incredulous. "Cuz you the one in hell, not him!"

"Stop it, Gladys," Aunt Malaika hisses. Her face looks strained, sweat running all around her eyes. She pulls the hem of her too-little shirt down and smooths it, wipes her brow with the sleeve. "That's enough from you. It's way too musty up in here without all your hot air, too."

Grey Eyes pursed her lips and closed her eyes, her whole neck and face frowned up with disapproval.

"Yeah," Miss Thin says, between sobs. "We not gon' talk about why you here, now are we?"

"No, we're not," Aunt Malaika says, cutting Grey Eyes off before she even got started again. "Seem like you two would get tired of fussing and fighting. Even the devil tired of hearing all y'all's mess. Ain't none of us going nowhere."

The three women sat with this in silence. Finally, Miss Thin wiped her eyes.

"Well, at least we have this nice young thing to keep us company," she said, perking up.

"Velma, she ain't here to stay. She just visiting, and in fact, she 'bout to go," Aunt Malaika says, struggling to stand up. Baffled, I hold her by her elbow, and let her lean on my shoulder as she gets to her feet. She's reaching a bare toe across the floor, looking for her slippers.

"Come on child," she said, hurried. "Wouldn't want you to miss your bus."

"But Aunt Malaika, I just got here, and we ain't hardly talked," I say as she dusts me off and straightens my loose shoulder strap. Suddenly, I feel like the floor been swept from underneath me. Why she rushing me out now?

"Mildred, we done said all that we need to say. You look good, so I guess, hard as it was, I done good," she says, brushing her hard knuckles against my cheek. She looks at me with something I've never seen from her before: satisfaction.

"You always was a good child, but so scared of stepping on your own shadow, I couldn't hardly get you to stand on your own feet." She stared up into my face, searching. "But you standing now, ain't you? And now you must go. Visiting hours should be just about up."

"Well, if you don't want her to stay, you better get her out of here," Miss Grey Eyes Gladys says. "'Cause when that heffa come with those pills . . ."

Aunt Malaika sighs. "I know." She turns to me. "Come on, Mildred, give your mama a kiss."

I look at her, feeling both guilt and relief. I move to the door, hurriedly, before her mood changes—or she changes her mind. I'm her daughter. That's what she said. In fact, she said it twice. No turning back from that. She satisfied.

"Should I come back, sometime next week? Next Sunday?"

She pats a loose braid and places it smoothly behind her ear. Her fingers have a marked tremor. We have the exact same ears, shaped like little rose petals. Why didn't I notice that before?

She looks troubled. "Baby, if you like. But you got to go now. And Mildred . . ."

"Yes?" I say, standing at the door. She reaches out, and for a moment, I think she will hug me, but she grasps my wrists. Her hands are cold—deadly cold. The shock of it makes me pull away, but she holds on. "Don't look behind you," she says, staring at me until I understand. "Remember."

#

Forget what they tell you. Hell is very small, and crowded. The ceilings are low and the hallways are narrow. A full-bodied soul like me can't hardly make no elbow room. And the air, the air smells like pot liquor and cooking grease, like something holed up in a smoky kitchen, while my Aunt Malaika sits on her bunk bed by a wavering window, staring at a strip of green, receding.

I walk quickly through the winding corridors, my eyes averted, my hands resting at my sides as I pass through the gates. I am holding my breath. I am not holding back tears. I am concentrating on white roses, sharp elbows resting in a dusty windowsill, I am thinking of my mother and I don't look back.

BELLY SPEAKER
BY
NICOLE KURTZ

The sharp New Mexican wind lodged grit in the corners of her mouth. She wiped her lips with the back of her sleeve and spat onto the dirt. Morning broke the horizon. She squinted against the shimmering light. All around, the desert landscape changed like so many towns before with tall poles and colorful canopies, exotic wildlife, and strange odors. Tucked into the crook of Honey's arm, Momma Wynn watched with unblinking eyes as the rainbow of tents sprouted up against the flushed sky. Early morning laborers' grunts and shouts broke the new day's quiet. Fires snapped and crackled from makeshift pits. Smoke wafted across the field, snaking across the grounds, seeking freedom.

"Honey! Git over 'ere and lend a hand. Ya know Anna's wit' child!" The carnival owner, Bob Mathers, gestured his meaty and chapped hands toward Anna, swollen and pink, who rubbed the small of her back.

"I'm practicing." Honeysuckle adjusted Momma Wynn against her knee, and then gestured with her head to the doll.

"Practicing what? How hard is it to make that stupid log of wood talk? Git over 'ere," Bob barked.

Don'tcha go over to 'em. Bloated pale pig.
Momma Wynn's hoarse voice held hints of anger.

"You say somethin'?" Bob crossed his arms across his round belly and glared. "Eh?"

"Nothing!" Honeysuckle squinted at Momma Wynn and met her glass glare. In a whisper, she added, "Shush you. He the boss. We the workers."
You the slave and he the massa.

"We ain't slave no more. Thank ya, Mr. Lincoln, God rest his soul. We found freedom doin' this work. Now come on. No rockin' the boat." Honeysuckle sighed and sat Momma Wynn down beside her chair before heading over to the carnival owner.

People crawled around—some she knew, some she didn't. Honeysuckle found comfort in strangers. Her dark robe brushed the tops of her boots as she walked. Her steps fell in a shush across the desert floor but shot little dusty clouds in her wake.

Even once she reached Big Bob, she could hear Momma Wynn whispering in her mind. *Don listen to 'em. Don't listen to 'em. Devils! Demons!*

"You walk so slow, lazy ass." Bob grunted and started toward the big tent. "Hercules could use some help with the cages."

Honeysuckle let it go, as her people had practiced doing for decades, letting the rancid bark of those supposedly superior flow from their scarred and marred backs. Holding her head high, she reached Hercules.

"Big man."

"Witch." He rumbled in greeting as he stood tall against the rising sun. Already drenched with sweat, he pushed a punishing hand through his shoulder-length hair. A mountain of a man, Hercules hadn't been his real name. After the war, everyone became someone else, even the nobodies. Carnival work gave them labels, allowed them to become strong men, funny men, belly speakers.

"I told you not to call me that." Honeysuckle reached down for the sledgehammer. "My momma was killed by witchcraft."

"Ah." Hercules had a sheen of anxious sweat dripping down his forehead. A hulking dark figure, he reached out for the sledgehammer. Callused rough hands waved her toward him. "Gimme, *witch.*"

He smirked outright, fleshing out a dimple. If he hadn't been so cruel, he might've been handsome.

A cold chill filtered up from her belly, gushing like a geyser inside her.

Thack!

She swung the heavy sledgehammer with ease, as if she had an extra set of hands. Honeysuckle watched the scarlet wound blossom across Hercules' upper chest, at the base of his throat, where the hammer's chipped edge snared his tanned flesh. The red stain inked its way through his thick fingers, clawing at his throat, dark eyes bulging as he fought to breathe.

Round, unblinking eyes took it all in.

"You don't hear too good. Do ya?" The sledgehammer smacked the dirt as it slid from Honeysuckle's grasp.

The icy burn began to recede, and as it did, she came back to herself. Her limbs tingled with pinpricks as if she'd been out in the cold too long. At once, Bob's shouting and Hercules' wheezing screams rent the dry air, and the thundering of running feet joined.

"What the hell you doin?" Bob shoved Honeysuckle aside. "Here! Here! Anna, get the doc!"

Honeysuckle's belly balled into a knot of gnawing fear. *What happened?*

She stumbled forward, tripping over the hammer's handle but catching herself before she hit the ground.

Bob snatched himself around to her, red-faced and spitting, fat bushy eyebrows crouched down in fury over angry, beady eyes. "You ain't right in the head. Gitoutta my sight! Where the hell is Doc? Herc'sturnin' blue!"

Honeysuckle pushed through the thin crowd and marched back to her trailer, scooped up Momma Wynn, and retreated to its comforts. Inside, the oily smell of kerosene overpowered the scents of old tomes and the passage of time. The lantern's soft glow cast shadows into heavy curtains and worn, leather-bound books. She plopped down on the edge of her bed and grabbed a bottle of whiskey from the floor beside. As she fingered the capped mouth, the amber liquid sloshed about half empty.

Just like Honeysuckle.

"What happened?"

Honeysuckle whirled around to Momma Wynn sitting on the loveseat.

The miniature doll with its hand-painted clothing, shoes, and facial features shook and began to grow. The wood rings pulsated in hypnotic fashion. Her soulless eyes widened, as did she—long wooden legs stretched out until the four-toed feet touched the throw rug. Lanky, thin, branch-like arms creaked as she reached out with four-fingered hands. The oblong head swelled "til it reached the ceiling. Leafy branches sprouted around her head to create a verdant afro.

Her lipless mouth opened, and Momma Wynn spoke. "Nothin'."

"Nothin'! He could die! If Hercules dies, Imma be headed for the noose, and you to the fire."

"Squashin' a bug. Riddin' the area of pests. Nothin' more." The gravelly voice clashed with Momma Wynn's faux cheery face. Somehow it made her words more sinister.

Honeysuckle swallowed to ease her dry throat before trying again.

"There's a big difference between bugs and people."

Momma Wynn's shimmering laughter shook her leaves, making them rustle in the small space, forcing the shadows to flicker. It raised gooseflesh along Honeysuckle's arms and tightened the knot in her belly.

Ever since she could remember, she'd had Momma Wynn. The wooden doll had spoken to her when she'd been old enough to fetch water from the well back in Tennessee, but never had she been in such a predicament as this. With mounting fear, Honeysuckle gaped at Momma Wynn, reclining on the loveseat unabashed. The grinning mouth, stretched to accommodate the now larger face, mocked Honeysuckle's fury. At the moment, all Honeysuckle could do was wait.

"Momma, we can't just attack a white man, even all the way out here! There's gonna be hell to pay, even if Hercules don't die."

"Ain't nobody gonna call me outta my name. Not no more."

"He didn't. He was talkin' to me..."

"Same as talkin' to me."

"But, Momma..."

"Hush now, chile."

#

A series of shouts and the sounds of laborers outside jolted Honeysuckle awake. Through bleary eyes and a pounding headache, she looked over to Momma Wynn. Though still seated on the loveseat, the doll's feet were now suspended high above the throw rug. Honeysuckle closed her eyes and breathed through the thundering at her temples. How'd she read the stars so wrong? Joining up with Bob's Traveling Circus had given her a place to stay, a way to see the country, and money, her own freedom. She peered over at Momma Wynn. Had she really achieved that freedom? Yeah, from bondage and servitude, sure. Although never alone, she *was* alone all the time. Momma Wynn didn't like people, especially those being friendly with Honeysuckle. The doll had helped her ice over the grief of her momma's death and helped her talents as a belly speaker grow. But, the doll had also crept up inside of her and torn a hole that she couldn't fix.

"My head feels in pain. I hate this."

"No, you don't. You just ain't use to what you like." Momma Wynn snickered.

"I know this is wrong!" Honeysuckle climbed to her feet, using the bed as leverage. Held down by her side, her fist shook as she stepped closer to the smirking dummy. The big painted-on smile and those wide, unblinking eyes stared straight ahead. It infuriated Honeysuckle.

"It's better to feel pain than nothin' at all."

Honeysuckle pulled back her hand from where she'd reached for Momma Wynn. The doll laughed. Despite the mirth, it held warning.

"How would you know? You don't feel anything! Just a stupid dummy." Honeysuckle crossed her arms in a huff. Momma Wynn had a way of reducing her from her twenty-five years to twelve.

"Your bones gonna be dust, forgotten and absorbed into the black earth, soon enough. Take pleasure in sufferin'! That's all there is anyway."

"Just cause my skin is dark don' mean Imma just lay down and die. Yeah, we suffer, Momma, but we live too. We fight hard, but we rise up and live. Imma keep on livin'."

Honeysuckle sighed as the cool springs rose from her belly, filtering through her body, like rushing waters. She'd pushed too far.

"Momma..." She hated how it sounded so much like a whine. "Somehow, you make me feel like I can't live without you, and I'm big enough now to get on."

"Out here folks live by the loaded gun. Only one gonna defend ya and keep ya safe, baby girl. *Me*."

A shudder rocketed through Honeysuckle. Momma Wynn's words rattled around inside her, down into her empty belly where all manner of darkness swirled, or so she imagined. Thanks to Momma Wynn, she could never trust her own eyes. The magic altered how she saw things. Honeysuckle knew there was something beyond *this*.

I can get away from her, but...

Banging interrupted her thoughts.

"Honey! Open this blasted door 'fore I tear it off!" Bob's knocking shook the trailer.

"Comin'! I'm comin'." She dropped the empty whiskey bottle, and it clattered to the floor.

With her head full of regret, Honeysuckle went to the door and peered through the thin curtain. Sure enough, Bob's balding and sunburned head turned to face her.

"Open the door!"

With a sigh, she unlocked the door and retreated farther inside. If the mob wanted her, they'd have to come in and get her. She wasn't gonna make it easy for them. The trailer sagged under Bob's weight. He squeezed into the tiny room, filling it with the odor of sweat and filth. He got almost to the loveseat before he quit trying to get closer.

Honeysuckle climbed to the rear of her bed where a small window rested at her back. Crouched on her heels, she held Momma Wynn in one hand. The roaring in her ears grew louder, and Momma Wynn's whispered chuckle served as an unsettling undercurrent. The air hung heavy with tension.

"What you want?" Honeysuckle clutched the doll tighter, and her skin grew colder.

"Now, Honey, ain'tnothin' to be frightened 'bout." He shot her a greasy smile. "Old Herc's gonna live. May not talk again, but he'll live."

Honeysuckle held her breath and waited for the rest. Experience had taught her that white men always repaid in kind what they perceived as defiance. The pull of the icy blackness welled up from her belly and pressed against her lips. She kept her mouth closed, but the pressure continued to build.

Bob's beady eyes shifted down to the doll and then back to Honeysuckle. "You, uh, use magic for that thing, huh? To make it talk?"

Honeysuckle shook from the freezing cold that exploded inside of her. The corners of her trailer went white. Frost crawled up the windows behind her, and her breath escaped in puffs. The kerosene lanterns flickered in warning. Suddenly laughter spilled out of her. Chills skated along her flesh in concert with the stream of maniacal mirth. Across from her, Bob scowled in confusion, at first, and then took a pained step backward, clearly un-nerved.

"Where you goin'?"

The voice's coarseness shocked Bob, and he glanced down to Momma Wynn.

"You heard me. Why the rush to run?"

His head snapped up to Honeysuckle. "Shut that dummy up 'fore it git you hurt."

Honeysuckle swallowed but held her lips shut. Truth was, she couldn't open them if she tried.

"Just, uh, keep yourself to yourself. Ya hear me?" With that, Bob squeezed out of the wagon so fast he snared his sleeve on the door's latch. He cursed and banged around the door's frame before disappearing into the blushing morn.

But the tone of his voice had held warning.

"That's it?" Honeysuckle blinked in disbelief.

She already had her answer. That wasn't the end. No way they would leave her unscathed after she attacked Hercules. Her reckoning had only been postponed. The West stayed wild despite all the attempts to tame it, claim it, and abuse it. A fierce rejection of conformity. This wide expanse of nothing held a kinship with Momma Wynn—barren and unyielding. Perhaps that's why Momma Wynn was so strong out here.

"Imma go out. Get food. I'm starvin'." Honeysuckle picked up her rifle and took a breath.

She glanced over to the doll and awaited the rebuke.

Silence.

Honeysuckle headed out into the yucca-scented air of a new day.

#

In the arid, high desert, few animals stirred this early. Honeysuckle pointed her rifle at the dawn and marched across the open space in search of food. Soon she happened upon a group of rodent-like animals, peeking out of a mound. It seemed some stood as sentries watching out for bigger predators, like her. She crouched down slowly and remained still. Bob called them prairie dogs and told her to keep it to herself. Although the idea of eating dog turned her stomach, Bob had assured her that they tasted gamy and weren't real dog. Now, she had to shoot one because her hunger was so real even the yucca looked tasty. It'd make a solid morning meal. From this distance, the camp's din punctured the quiet. The aroma of roast meat wafting from their campgrounds made her belly growl and her mouth water.

The wind whipped about something fierce, driving some of the prairie dogs back into their mound. They weren't the only ones on the prowl. Once the wind died, the heavy shuffle of feet snared her attention. Honeysuckle rose from the sparse brush, rifle in hand.

"Who's there?"

The wind roared again, stealing some of her words, but not her rising alarm. The hunter turned prey. A way of life for women in the West and in these lawless times.

A few feet away, Bob and a cluster of dusty men stopped. The two on horseback wore cowboy hats and apathetic glares. Bob and Hercules stood, horseless. The animals whinnied in greeting. They must've followed her, tracked her like an animal through the brush. Hercules carried a thick rope in one hand, and an angry scowl marred his face. The deep purple bruise across his neck spoke louder than any words he could say. That shut him up. The others wore gun belts slung low on their waists.

A lynch mob.

She warned Momma Wynn this would happen. Reckoning would come, and as always with men, so would violence.

"Go easy, Honey." Bob gestured with his fat left hand for her to lower her weapon.

"Mornin' again, Bob. Gentlemen." Honeysuckle sweetened her words but kept her rifle raised. The familiar feeling in her belly stirred.

"You know why I'm here." Bob nodded at Hercules. "We gotta make this right."

The others grunted in agreement.

"You sayin' my apology ain't enough?" Honeysuckle shuddered as the iciness flowed throughout her person. The wind picked up, again, but she held her weapon firm. Her fingers ached.

"Now, Honey, you attacked, hell, damn near killed 'em." Bob jerked a thumb at Hercules. "Ain't no savage gonna harm my crew. We can't have that kind of doin' 'round 'ere. We civilized folk."

"Ask the Indian 'bout that," Honeysuckle whispered.

"What? Speak up!" Bob moved closer, but still out of striking distance. "Quit ya mumbling."

Honeysuckle trained the gun on him. "No closer or she bangs."

The men on horseback drew their guns. At this, she finally took them in. Two shiny stars had been pinned to their shirts—a sheriff and a deputy.

Four men.

Three guns.

Two horses.

One Honeysuckle.

As the rising panic pressed against her throat, she squeezed her fingers tighter around the rifle, but she couldn't make them stop trembling.

Ain't no man gonna hurt my baby.

"Momma..."

The ache eased from her fingers, and a cool calm settled over her. She sighed as the internal whispers offered assurance and comfort. Nothing to fear. Momma promised she'd protect her. A low drone, a hum of laughter, rippled up from her belly.

"Now, dontcha go beggin' for ya ma. You hurt Herc. The sheriff here says that's a hangin' offense." Bob adjusted his pants and gun belt.

Behind him, on the gray horse, the thin sheriff tipped his hat and spat a wad of tobacco. Thin rivulets of brown streamed down his chin into his beard. His pistol remained in his hand, ready to render judgment.

"You ain't got no arrest papers, no jury or trial. This is still America." Honeysuckle swallowed. "And I have rights now. Not as many as you, but I got 'em."

The men chuckled, then sobered.

"Out here, all this openness. Who gonna find ya?" Bob asked, wiping the sweat from his face.

"Who'd care?" the sheriff snorted.

"One less blackie to bother us," the other added with a shrug.

"Killing me kills your profit. I bring a fair bit of coin to you, paying customers who like my show." Honeysuckle knew her act provided good attendance. Curious people loved her "exotic" looks and the strangeness of her belly speaking abilities. They'd often try to touch her hair, her skin, and of course, Momma Wynn. Honeysuckle didn't like equating her life's worth with money— it happened all too often to her people—but that seemed to be all men like Bob understood.

Your grace is wasted on 'em.

Bob paused and studied her as he stroked his double chins.

The others' hard chuckles tapered off, and in the void, silence swelled.

Your good heart gonna get you chewed up.

"Ain't you got somethin' to say, Hercules?" The words thundered, spooking the men.

"Who said that?" Bob asked, looking around, pistol slicing through the air as he waved it.

"Don't all you menfolk got all the answers?" the same voice jeered.

"She said it!" The sheriff nodded at Honeysuckle.

"Nuh uh. Her lips didn't move," the deputy countered.

They looked around, at each other, and then back to Honeysuckle. No one else had arrived. She hadn't moved. Instead, Honeysuckle held Hercules' dark, angry gaze. The voice clearly wasn't hers.

"Oh. You can't, can you?" She smirked, but not on her own accord.

Hercules lunged at her, and she fired... wide. It was enough to force the sheriff and his deputy to return fire.

Confusion erupted around them as Momma Wynn's anger rose. A crack of electricity made the deputy's horse whinny and collapse to the ground, rolling onto the man's leg. Agonized howls joined the chorus of shouts and cursing.

Hercules dropped to the ground and tossed his arms over his head.

Bob shouted in fury and with fist raised, spun to face the sheriff. "Ya almost shot me!"

"Shut up! She's gettin' away!"

"Ma leg! Ma leg!" the deputy screamed.

Honeysuckle ran, scattering the prairie dogs and other creatures as she fled. She'd used her talent for mischief before, but this time it may have saved her life.

#

The tiny fire's flames licked at the skinned rabbit with eagerness. Still daylight, Honeysuckle hunched down in an abandoned hogan, a home the Diné had used as a dwelling. Perhaps they'd had nothing left to fight for so they'd pushed on. Or were too weary of war. Honeysuckle had collected tumbleweeds and wood pieces scattered around the truncated trees to make a feeble fire. After that, she'd managed to catch a rabbit, snapping its neck to avoid alerting Bob to her location. Her hunting knife did the rest. The fire's smoke only spoke to an occupant, not necessarily her. Still, an anxiousness settled around her. Each animal scuttling and twig snapping made her jump.

Full, with greasy fingers still tender from pinching the searing meat, Honeysuckle blew out a breath. She couldn't stay here forever. Momma Wynn waited, as did the rest of her own belongings, back in her trailer. With her fear in full bloom, she didn't dare chance a return without a plan. For now, the fizzing ceased inside, but everything felt just beyond her grasp.

She rubbed her arms, but it offered little ease from the raw anxiety crawling across her skin. Using the last stores of energy she had, she stood and peered out across the New Mexican landscape. The setting sun flushed the horizon with pinks and oranges. Such a glorious place for such ugly things to occur.

But she and chaos were old friends. Her life's map bore many memories of conflict and close calls. Each time, Momma Wynn had been there, an ever-present pillar of maternal strength. This time Honeysuckle would have to be bold, and her boldness would need to stand alone.

But did she have to do it alone?

Don't underestimate the things Imma do, Momma Wynn had told her more than once. The dummy's protection had saved Honeysuckle, too. Momma Wynn's cold sensations left her feeling hollow like this hogan.

Why battle alone against the mob? Across the flat land, Honeysuckle glimpsed something in the falling light. Almost at once, she blended back into the hogan's shadows cloaking herself in its darkness. The rustling grew louder as the minutes ticked by. She crawled over to the fire where her pack rested and fished out her hunting knife. Her rifle would announce her location to others, but she picked it up anyway. The blade would do but having both made her feel prepared. She scurried back to her previous position by the door.

The wind stilled and thickened with each breath. A thatch of cacti shuddered moments before the wooden doll emerged. Momma Wynn. Some rogue debris stuck to her hair and clothing, but she reached the outer edge of the yard.

"Momma!" Honeysuckle dropped the weapons and raced out to retrieve her.

Once she scooped the doll up, the cold crawling inside her returned. Despite this, she was comforted.

"Be calm," Momma Wynn whispered.

"How'd you get here? How'd you find me?" Honeysuckle searched the surroundings. No one. She pivoted back inside with her heart pounding.

Stunned, she sat down beside the fire. As she plucked the debris out of Momma Wynn's hair, she peered at the doll's short wooden legs.

"Momma?"

"Yeah?"

"How'd you find me?" Honeysuckle's mouth had gone dry.

"I'll find you no matta where ya go. We one." Momma Wynn laughed as if the question was ridiculous.

It raised chills across Honeysuckle's arms. "What that mean?"

Honeysuckle cradled Momma Wynn in her lap, both facing the fire. Momma Wynn's head suddenly turned 180 degrees to face Honeysuckle.

"I men' what I said. We gonna be together always."

Momma Wynn's painted-on mouth jeered at her.

"What if I find a man I like?"

"Then you find him dead."

Honeysuckle froze. An impulse to throw Momma Wynn into the flames shot through her. It might sever the tethered link between them. Would she wither if their link did? She squeezed the dummy. She just didn't know. One toss and drop, then it would be all over. A moment of hesitation made her hands shake.

With a sigh, she set Momma Wynn down beside her in the dirt. The twisted head didn't sit right with her.

Momma Wynn righted herself and then stretched out—her hair becoming leaves, limbs lengthening to adult size. Momma Wynn became more, a full tree of life. Now, as big as Honeysuckle, Momma Wynn scooted away from the fire, as if she knew Honeysuckle's previous dark thoughts. Honeysuckle couldn't ever be sure. Their bond left them tethered physically, but how else did Momma Wynn find her? Sometimes, Honeysuckle suspected the doll could read her mind, too. Momma Wynn had taken control of her body before, so why not her mind?

At this, a chill skated over Honeysuckle.

"You think you gonna be done with me." It wasn't a question, but a heated declaration. "You want your freedom."

"I do."

Not until that moment did it solidify for Honeysuckle that she *did*. She'd never liked being shackled. Once she secured her freedom, she was loath to lose it. Although Momma Wynn had brought her success and a job, she'd also cost her. Honeysuckle's life was too high a price to pay for Momma Wynn's temper. If Momma Wynn killed any or all of the men in the mob, then things would only be worse. Momma Wynn's unpredictable nature threatened any chance Honeysuckle would have for a safe and normal life.

"Not gonna happen." Momma Wynn's branches rustled in warning. "We gonna be together always."

"You don't want me to be happy."

"Thought you'd be happy breathin'," Momma Wynn mocked.

Honeysuckle glowered and crossed her arms in a huff. Across the fire pit, Momma Wynn chuckled at her pout.

"Only me gonna save ya."

"I don't need savin'." Honeysuckle grunted at the hard resentment staining each of those words. The boast sparked an idea inside her, but instead of speaking it aloud, she tucked it away for later.

"Yeah, you do." Momma Wynn rose and moved around the circle, closer to Honeysuckle.

"Savin' is for sinners." Honeysuckle stood up.

"You ain't no saint."

"You ain't neither."

Momma Wynn's leaves rustled in the ensuing silence, but she didn't jeer. No snapping comeback. Maybe she heard the resolve in Honeysuckle's voice.

Good. Honeysuckle grinned. It felt good to stand on her own feet.

As the day bled to night, Honeysuckle wondered how long before Momma Wynn knocked her to her knees.

Or Bob hanged her by the neck.

#

The crisp New Mexican wind whipped Honeysuckle rubbed the sleep out of her eyes with one thought. *Water.* Clutching her knife, it took several fast blinks before she oriented herself. She took in the shadowy and strange surroundings with fear pumping through her. The blackened fire pit still sent a thin trail of smoke into the air. It stained the room with the scent of burnt hair and soot. Farther away, between the pit and the entrance, Momma Wynn lay face down in the dirt.

The wind wasn't the only thing that snatched her awake. Crunching of boots on dirt and snapping twigs alerted her through sleep's thin veil to something approaching. With her hunting knife, she stood up and crept to the sole window. On tiptoes, she peered out into the new day. Just before dawn, only a sliver of sunlight provided illumination. Figures stumbled around in the gloom. Their lanterns bobbed like fat junebugs lazily bouncing in the air. The curses sounded human enough.

Darn it! They found her.

She had minutes, maybe, to plan a way out. She rubbed the remainder of sleep from her eyes with the back of her blouse. As she stepped back, she tripped over Momma Wynn. She caught herself, and she stared down at the dummy. Honeysuckle braced for the familiar belly speaker to start.

No cold inkling erupted inside.

"Momma?" she whispered.

Nothing. Only the rawness of her own terror. A strangely new emotion that made her a bit ill.

"Honey!" Bob shouted and brought her back to the situation.

"Come on outta there."

Honeysuckle gripped the knife's hilt tight, thought about the number of pistols out there, and picked up her rifle. The round space made her a sitting duck. Trapped, it was too late to leave. Swearing, Honeysuckle pressed herself flat against the wall beside the entrance. With luck, she'd be able to take out a couple of them before she died. She'd go down fighting, not on her knees pleading for mercy.

The first man inside caught the rifle butt with his face. He howled and swung blindly. Thankful for her dark skin, she blended into the shadows. When her assailant stalked by her, unaware, she swung, and then ducked into the next patch of shadow. She repeated this several times, extending the element of surprise. The narrow entrance forced them to enter one at a time.

"Git her!" the sheriff howled.

Honeysuckle rolled across the dirt and tripped the second man. Easy enough, since he dragged one of his legs. He fell on top of the other man. The deputy's youthful voice coughed out a groan. The men's frustrated shouts as they struggled to untangle themselves amused her.

"That's enough, Honey." Bob's tone made Honeysuckle's pause.

She stood up and turned to face him. He held a pistol in one hand and a lantern in the other. An oily grin emerged from the dark stubble crawling across his double chins.

"Git on up now." Bob pushed his girth farther into the space and directed her with the gun.

Hercules silently followed behind and squeezed into the narrow available space.

"This is a real shit hole, innit?" Bob barked out a laugh.

Bob and Hercules threatened on her left, the sheriff and the deputy to her right. She couldn't see a way out, but then the cold burst blossomed up from her belly. Honeysuckle shuddered, not in fear nor from cold, but rather from Momma Wynn's full fury.

"Beware."

That simple word thundered.

"Who said that?" Bob searched around.

"My belly's speakin'," Honeysuckle explained. "You oughta listen."

Hercules' pinched and pained expression conveyed his anger. The dawn's light illuminated the inside of the hogan and the men therein. They put their lanterns down in the dust.

"She doin' it again," the deputy stammered as he got to his feet. He held hand to the left side of his head, where blood trickled between his fingers. He'd been sent in first.

"A trick. Nothin' more," Bob countered.

At this, the wind roared through the hogan so powerful it blew off the cowboys' hats. Momma Wynn's power unraveled in the confined area, stirring up dust in hungry gusts.

Momma's coming.

As soon as she thought it, the air shifted.

Spooked, the sheriff shot toward the exit. "Gi-toutta my way!"

Bob blocked the door, and the sheriff shoved at the mass. He failed to move the huge man. Bob didn't budge. "You ain't leaving'."

Roughly the same height as Bob, the sheriff leaned in close and poked him with his own gun. "You gonna stop me? Didn't think so."

Without waiting for a reply, he wedged himself through a sliver of space and out of the hogan.

The deputy bolted, too. "Ain't worth this witch-craft shit."

"Buncha yells-bellied bastards!" Bob shouted after them before turning his attention back on Honeysuckle. "Welp, the law ain't here, so we ain't gonna follow any rules now, Herc."

The wind began again. Coupled with the laughter, wild and evil. Honeysuckle's insides froze. Wincing, she struggled to stay conscious. Bob and Hercules staggered as the world shook. They toppled over onto each other. Once one man hit the ground, weeds scrambled up from the earth. They pinned the men against the dirt and choked them. Gagging sounds rose up against the day. Honeysuckle fought the frost from consuming her by trying to stay awake. If she blacked out, she'd fail. Momma Wynn threatened to take over, and she'd kill them. The vegetation coiled around their necks. Their faces paled before turning to shades of blue. The men's gurgling faded as Momma Wynn sucked the life out of them.

Honeysuckle staggered over to the men. Momma Wynn's roaring laugh echoed in malicious glee.

"Not again!" Honeysuckle couldn't tolerate the callous disregard for life any longer.

"They mean to kill ya. Let them die!" The wind whirled in greater intensity, crushing the life out of them. Momma Wynn controlled everything, even *her*. Now. This was the time. If Bob and Hercules died, there would be more bounty on her head. Not only that, but their deaths would resolve nothing. She wanted to be in control of her life.

"Stop!" Honeysuckle's heart thundered in her chest, and it burned, hot in outrage. "Enough!"

She screamed so loud, it pulled from the depths of her being. It shot through her like a geyser, flooding her with fire. Honeysuckle raced to the men and began tearing at the weeds. As she tore through the restraints, not only those from the ground, but also inside herself, she beat back the icy feeling. It retreated with each snap. The yuccas cut and scratched her skin, tearing at her flesh with eager defiance. She grinned at the pain, and the cold recoiled further back into her belly.

What you doin? Momma Wynn shrieked. Panic stretched the words thin.

"I'm gettin' back my voice!" Honeysuckle grunted.

"Let me up!" Bob yelled. He thrashed about, his pudgy parts flailed against his bonds and strained against them. They didn't yield.

Honeysuckle crawled over to her hunting knife where it'd been discarded in the whirlwind. She hurried back to Bob and Hercules and sliced through the vegetation. Covered in dirt and slashes, Bob lumbered to his booted feet. Beside him, Hercules scurried back from her, got to his feet, and fled.

"Honey?" Bob croaked, rubbing his neck beneath his fleshy chins. He then patted his holster for his pistol, but it lay several feet away. His eyes darted to Honeysuckle as realization dawned across his face. He licked his lips.

"Shut. It." She stood up and poked him in the flabby folds of his chest. "Imma go and you ain't gonna follow me. Ever. Got it?"

Bob opened his mouth but closed it quick. Instead, he nodded before walking out the hogan, grumbling under his breath.

After he left, Honeysuckle picked up her rifle, sheathed her knife, and shouldered her satchel. A numbness took up residence inside her. Momma Wynn's familiar cold comfort had gone. With a glance down at the broken and battered doll, Honeysuckle took in a deep, steadying breath. Now, she'd do the next shows of her life alone. It felt both strange and exciting. An internal quiet made her uneasy, but in time, she'd adjust.

At last she'd found her voice.

Her belly would speak for her no longer.

The End

Blacktastic

SOUTHERN COMFORT
BY
VALJEANNE JEFFERS

Nandi sat on her porch sipping her coffee, a tall brown woman, her short hair curled about her head. She watched as dawn's blush filled the sky with blue and orange glory. Beyond the trees, across from her wooden house, she could see the river. Blossoming herbs intermingled with azaleas flowered in her yard. It was already 70 degrees, the day promising to be hot and humid. Nandi took another sip of her coffee and frowned. Irie would be stopping by, and she never knew what to expect from her daughter's visits.

She glimpsed the hants moving about her porch and smiled warmly. A long-legged, ebony-colored spirit sat down in the chair beside her. "Morning Cecil," she said. He nodded in greeting.

A buxom woman appeared on the porch steps. She looked back at Nandi and smiled. "Morning, Peaches," Nandi greeted her.

"Morning, Miss Nandi."

She heard the children's laughter, looked to the right, and saw them making their way up the dirt road. Her grandsons, six-year-old Derrick and four-year-old Calvin, small and dark like their mother, ran ahead of Irie. At the sound of their chatter the spirits chuckled softly and hid themselves in the foliage.

"Hey Grandma!" Derrick exclaimed. He ran up the stairs to hug her, Calvin close on his heels.

She embraced the boys. "Hey baby ... hey sugar." But her eyes were on her daughter. Nandi's face tightened in anger, as she spotted the reddish bruise on Irie's cheek that she'd tried to conceal with makeup. The spirits hissed in refrain, a sound like angry hornets. "Quiet!" she hissed. They fell silent.

Irie looked into her mother's eyes, and quickly looked away. "Morning mama, I came by to get that twenty you promised me."

"Good morning. Where's Jimmy?"

Irie twisted her mouth. "He at work," she said defensively. "Where you think he at this time of the morning?"

"Y'all had breakfast?" Nandi asked.

"Ain't no food in the house."

Nandi sucked her teeth. "He will work," she muttered. "But I sho' don't know what he does with his money."

"If it's a problem," Irie bristled, her dark eyes flashing "that's alright."

Nandi's face softened. "Come on in the house; let me fix y'all some breakfast."

"I want pancakes, Grandma!" Derrick exclaimed. He turned to his younger brother. "Don't you want some pancakes?"

Calvin nodded emphatically. "Uh-huh!"

Nandi pushed up from her rocker. "Well, come on then."

In the kitchen, Nandi poured a cup of coffee for her daughter, and busied herself stirring pancake batter. "Robert stopped by yesterday," she said.

Irie's face brightened. "What did he say?"

"Wish he had done all that asking when I was single."

"You never gave him a chance." Beside Nandi the spirits whispered in agreement.

"Well, it don't matter 'cause I'm married now. Mama can you give me something?"

Nandi looked up sharply. "Something like what? You pregnant again?"

"Naw, not for that ... something to help me and Jimmy get along better."

The older woman quirked her mouth and shook her head. She poured glasses of milk for the boys ... placed a plate of silver dollar pancakes on the table ... plates and folks. She pulled maple syrup down from the cabinet. "Gone on and eat. We'll talk later."

##

The boys finished eating. "Can we go outside, Mama?" Derrick asked.

"Yeah, stay on the porch."

"Aww!" they cried in unison.

"We'll be outside in a minute."

Nandi poured herself another cup of coffee, and refilled Irie's cup. "What he hit you for this time?"

Irie sighed tiredly, for a moment looking much older than her 26 years. "It was my fault. We were arguing about some girl he works with. He told me to hush—" "It ain't your fault that man can't keep his hands to himself!" Nandi blurted. The spirits swirled about, mirroring her rage, and the kitchen was plunged into darkness.

Irie fidgeted in her chair, glancing about uneasily. "Mama ...!"

Nandi let go of her rage, and quickly lowered her voice. The darkness vanished. "It *ain't* your fault. You hear me?"

Irie nodded. "Can you give me something, Mama?"

"We tried that already, remember? There ain't nothing I can give you to stop Jimmy."

"Why not?"

"Because it ain't in his *nature,* that's why. Jimmy don't want to change. He likes things just the way they are. He knows anytime he wants his way, all he got to do is pound on you."

Irie starred at her cup. Tears rolled down her face. The kitchen was bathed in a soft blue light, the spirits mirroring her sadness. "I can't believe that. I can't believe this is it ...that ain't nothing gonna change."

Nandi reached over and touched her daughter's hand. "Ain't nothing gonna change unless you change it baby."

Irie wiped her face with her hands. "You never liked Jimmy noway. That's why you won't help me, like you help everybody else."

"Naw, I ain't never liked him. I never liked men that beat on women."

"Nobody but my daddy, right?" Irie said scornfully. At the look of remembered pain on Nandi's face, Irie said, "Sorry, Mama."

"No need for sorry. Come on, let's go back outside." The women moved out onto the porch and sat in the wooden rockers. With a whoop of joy, the boys jumped down into the grass to play.

"You right, I did stay with your daddy," Nandi went on, a faraway look in her eyes, "even though he beat me. Maybe that's the reason why you fell so hard for Jimmy. He just like your daddy—even looks like him. But I put him out, Irie. He didn't die here. Not at my house. Sally Mae, that woman he took up with after I quit him, she was the one stabbed him to death."

"Folks say you the reason she did that," Irie said softly.

Nandi shook her head. "I had nothing to do with it. I didn't need to root Sally to get her to kill him. She wanted to, and I don't blame her. If I hadn't quit him, I'd a wound up killing him myself."

Irie rocked slowly, watching her boys chase each other through the grass. "Give me something, Mama, *please.*"

"Alright, but just you remember what I told you. It ain't gonna do no good." Nandi got up and walked back inside. She continued through the living room to her kitchen and opened the door beside her gas stove. Here, lay her cupboard of magical unguents, the shelves stacked with folk medicine: charms and roots, powders and oils. She walked to the first shelf and picked up a jar of red powder.

A plume of smoke rose from the floor. And a banana-colored ghost, Isabelle, appeared inside. "It won't work."

"I know."

"Then what you giving it to her for?" Isabelle scoffed.

Nandi turned to look at the spirit. "Because she won't take my word for it. She got to learn for herself," she said in a tired voice. "Me telling her won't make a difference." She took another flowered jar from the shelf and fished out a twenty. Nandi hesitated a moment, and then pulled another bill from the jar.

"She borrowing money from you again, too. Might as well put it a bow-hog's butt and tell him to suey." Isabelle vanished.

##

"Here," Nandi handed her daughter the money. "This is forty." She pulled the jar from her pocket. "Put a tablespoon of this in his food. Be sure to make love to him the same night."

"Thank you, Mama. I'll give you the money back next week."

"Uh-huh." Nandi slowly rocked. She lifted her eyes from her grand-babies, gazing at the river beyond the trees.

##

Irie and children had already gone, when the youngest spirit appeared sitting beside her. Dolphus, a slender hant with a long scar running down his cheek. The angry one. "Why don't you let us take care of him?" His voice was a bass rumble, rattling the door and windows. "You know he ain't gonna stop."

"I don't want Jimmy's blood on my hands."

Peaches appeared, seated in midair to her left. "What about Irie—your grand-babies. He put her in the hospital last month. You gonna wait until he kills her?"

Nandi slowly rocked. "Before that happens she'll get tired. Just like I did."

##

The hard knock at her door jerked her from sleep. Twelve PM glowed on her wall clock. She flung the covers back and leaped out of bed. The knocking sounded again. *"Grandma!"* came Derrick's hysterical cry.

Nandi ran to the door and snatched it open. Derrick stood there, his face wet with tears. *"Grandma, he got a knife! Daddy got a knife!"*

Invisible to Derrick, the spirits that rose up behind her. Nandi threw her head back and screamed in the undulating wail of her ancestors. In answer, the trees were tossed by a great wind. She pulled the child to her, so he couldn't see the sudden flames burning inside her eyes.

"GO!" she cried, her voice like thunder. They surged pass her into the night, leaping and bounding up the road. Nandi scooped Derrick up in her arms and jumped from the porch. Still holding him, she loped behind them with preternatural speed—running faster than humanly possible—Derrick bouncing in her arms.

When she reached the house, the door was open. Inside, Irie lay on the floor, her face battered. The spirits had surrounded Jimmy, chunks of his flesh were disappearing as he screamed in pain and terror. The butcher knife lay forgotten at his feet. Calvin stood in the corner watching with eyes like saucers.

"You child—to *me!*" Nandi called. Calvin ran pass his father, and she picked him up with her free hand. Holding both children, she shouted: "Irie, let's *go!*" Irie got to her feet painfully, her wide eyes on her husband.

"Come on, gal!" Nandi urged. "When they hungry, they forget who's around!"

Irie turned her back on Jimmy and escaped into the night. His dying screams following her, fading as she made her way up the road to freedom.

HELLFIRE

BY

KENESHA WILLIAMS

It was September and the weather were cooling down, but in the annoying way where it would be sixty degrees when you woke up in the morning, eighty degrees in the middle of the day, and then back to sixty again at night. I normally woke up around sundown anyway, so I dressed for the lowest temperature of the day. I had on my uniform of black t-shirt, black chinos, and black boots on. I was a bouncer for a small upscale gentleman's club located in Northwest, Washington, DC. I loved my job. I got to flirt with pretty girls, keep people safe, and got one free drink a night. It sure beat night patrols in Afghanistan.

Archie's was pretty safe and one of the easiest bouncing gigs I'd done since I began my second career. The clients for the most part were businessmen letting off steam before they went home to their families. We sometimes got a Senator or Congressman in here, but that was usually around lunchtime when I was off, but sometimes they came at night.

If they were smart they stayed at one of their little frat boy like dorms at night and used a call in. Definitely not good for the general public to walk in and see Rep. John C. Smith (R) Wisconsin sitting down at the bar and stuffing Benjamin's in a strippers G-String. Every once in a while, a dude might get a little too tipsy and try and stretch the boundaries of what was proper with one of our ladies and then I'd nicely show him the door if I had inside duty or if I was on perimeter duty chase away some of the homeless guys that would harass the customers.

I'm a good guy so I usually peeled off a least a fiver and gave them a card to the nearest shelter. I knew that there for the grace of God go I. A lot of this city's homeless were vets just like me, I was just luckier than them. Had a good support system and a reliable therapist.

I leaned against the brick facade of *Archie's* and watched some of the girls come in for their shift. I was early, and I didn't have to be inside for another thirty minutes, but I'd gotten claustrophobic in the house. I just lived a couple of blocks from the club so even the walk here wasn't enough to winnow away some of the time.

"Hey hon," Sherry said as she hopped out of her Uber with her rolling trunk of costumes and makeup trailing behind her. "What's up, early ain't ya?"

"Wanted to see your beautiful face," I replied. The Uber driver honked loudly at us and stuck her head out, it was Sherry's girlfriend Malinda. She stuck out her pierced tongue at me.

"Keep your hands to yourself cabrón!" she yelled.

We all laughed at the old joke. Sherry was like a little sister to me and Malinda was like a sister-in-law. They were regulars over my house for my Sunday dinners. Yeah, handsome and a good cook, I'm a catch. Sherry poked her head back into the car and gave Malinda a good-bye kiss.

I envied them. Shit, I envied anyone who had a relationship longer than thirty days. That seemed to be my record lately.

"What's cooking for Sunday?" Malinda asked snapping me out of my own lonely ass thoughts.

"Pesto topped salmon sound good to you?"

"Hell yeah, see you Sunday!" With that she drove off probably to her next fare. It was Friday night and that meant prime Uber fare time downtown. All of the denizens, tourists, and day trippers were scurrying around the city in search of fine dining or nightlife right about now. The last of the commuters were safely tucked into their Metro train cars, save for the few who were hitting up the local happy hours before they made the one-hour ride back to Maryland or Virginia.

"Hey Terrance, I'ma put my stuff down then come back out to talk with you, okay?" Sherry asked. I shrugged my answer at her. Didn't want her to think I was lonely but didn't want to scare her off from coming back either.

I knew I shouldn't have come in today, but what else would I have done if I hadn't? Moped around in my apartment all day is what. It was coming up on five years, but on this day, it always felt like it was just yesterday. I thought I was going to be okay today. Seeing Sherry and Malinda so in love just brought it all back. No matter how hard I tried to distract myself, my brain kept coming back to the day someone murdered the love of my life.

I leaned against the brick wall in the alleyway and waited for Sherry to come back out. The alleys were usually rank around the clubs but suddenly I was smelling a stench that made my eyes water. I looked on the darkened alley to see where the smell was coming from but couldn't find the source.

Before I could locate the source of the smell, Sherry came out the club banging the hard metal door behind her. I turned to see her and then the shadow behind her began to elongate and stretch into a grotesque shape that was definitely not her shadow. The shadow then became flesh, if you could call it that, it looked like a quivering mass of shit shaped into a vaguely human form.

"Sherry watch out!" I screamed, but it was too late. The monster grabbed her and placed its hand over her mouth to stifle her scream. I rushed the figure and threw a punch that landed into what would be its face. My fist went through the entity like it was pudding. I recoiled at the sensation and hoped I'd be able to scrub the shit smell off of my hand eventually.

The monster threw Sherry to the ground where she landed with a loud thump that I knew must have knocked her out. Now, I was really mad I had no idea what I was up against, but my anger welled up in me and I was starting to get flashbacks to my wartime days. I reeled back to throw another punch, but what came out of me was a white-hot light or rather flame that burned towards the monster.

The monster was surprised and stepped back. Hell, I was surprised too, that had never happened before. The monster and I traded punches his heavy and smelly and mine with fire that didn't burn my fists but surprised the hell out of me with every punch I threw.

Even with my new-found powers I was starting to get tired and didn't sense the next punch that was coming towards me. I knew I couldn't' duck it, so I braced myself for the impact. It hurt like hell.

That punch had me on my knees and I could see the monster priming to throw another hard one towards my head. A haymaker that I didn't' think I'd be able to survive. Behind me a clanging like the clamor of a metal trashcan falling sounded. Was there someone there to help me. I wouldn't know because right then was when I passed out.

My first memory upon waking up was of Diana smacking the shit out of me from what I thought was a drunken stupor. Although at the time I didn't know her name was Diana and I didn't know how I'd gotten into her apartment. I figured she was just some one-night stand that was tired of me taking up space in her bright and cozy efficiency.

"Get up stupid," she said in an accent tinged with both British and Jamaican tones. I attempted to set up but winced at the pain that was radiating throughout my body. I don't know what kind of bender I was on or what I had done while on it, but it felt like somebody had beat the shit out of me.

"Fuck me," I said as I laid my head back on her plush velvet tufted couch. Diana pushed one of her long Sandy Brown dreadlocks out of her face and leaned in close to me.

"You smell like shit, why ya try ta chase down a level two demon by yourself? The Gorgon, really?" She paced around the small room at such a frenetic pace she'd given me a bigger headache than the one I already had.

"Demon? Listen hon I don't know what you're talking about I thought that we both came here to you know..."

"What are you trying to say you don't remember chasing the demon, don't remember getting the stuffing beat out of you, and then me coming and saving your ass?"

I shook my head in answer which just intensified the headache.

Diana threw her hands up in the air and started talking in a fast clip with some cursing thrown in for good measure. All I could make out was rasclass this and bombaclat that. Thinking back to the last vacation I had a couple of years ago where I took a cruise to Jamaica I knew that those weren't pleasant words.

She came back over to the couch where I laid down and looked me over with what I could only describe as the stink eye.

"You rest. I need to make some calls."

"Okay," I answered to her retreating figure. Looking at her small waist, full hips, and beautiful backside, I wished like hell she'd been a one-night stand instead of what I know knew she was, a gibbering loon. DC was full of crazy people and I dealt with them all the time being a bouncer. Never seen a crazy as fine as her though. She seemed pretty harmless besides the sailor's mouth, but if I had to listen to a chick cursing me out I'd definitely choose her pretty pout over anyone else's.

I settled down into the soft couch and tried to rest my sore body. Diana had gone into the bathroom to make her call, for privacy I guessed. I hoped she wasn't calling the cops on me, but suddenly I was too sleepy to care.

###

As I slept fitfully, I started to feel as if I was burning from the inside out. Flames hotter than the back draft from an IED engulfed my internal organs. I leaped from the couch and ran to the sink to find a way to temper the burning sensation that inflamed my insides. I turned on the faucet and put my mouth on the spigot letting the cold water run down my throat as well as my neck and chin. After swallowing what felt like a gallon of water I turned off the faucet.

My insides still felt like they were on fire and I looked around the small apartment looking for something else to assuage the heat. Looking around I found nothing that could help my plate but saw Diane leaning against a wall writing something in a small notebook. She had on glasses now that made her look more innocent than her mouth had earlier.

"What the Hell's going on?" I asked her afraid that she had slipped me something before I'd gotten here, and it was now making me feel like I had my very own campfire inside my body.

"I'm guessing hellfire," she said as if that were a perfectly normal thing to say.

"Lunatic!" I yelled at her. Intellectually I knew that yelling at someone who is actually crazy probably wasn't the best move, but I wasn't feeling sane myself at the moment.

"See if you can direct it out of your body, but don't burn any of my shit," she said. I cocked my eyebrow in a gesture that said you're shitting me, but I would do anything to get this damnable feeling out of me. So, I focused on the sink and extended my hands toward it and thought about getting whatever was in me out. Amazingly a stream of fire so hot that it was white leapt from my finger-tips into the still wet basin of the sink.

"Yep, hellfire," she said as she scribbled some-thing else into her little notebook.

"Look lady you're gonna have to tell me what's going on here," I said.

"You want the good news or the bad news?" she asked.

"So, the good news is your body has given you temporary amnesia to block out something that was obviously very very traumatic for you. The bad news is you need to get out the block to figure out what the Hells going on with you," she said.

I knew a little bit about your brain trying to pro-tect you from trauma, being an Afghanistan vet def-initely taught me about the ways that you'll perform mental gymnastics to get through something hellish but even with all that I saw on the battlefield I never had memory loss. I blinked slowly trying to make sense of what she was telling me especially since she sounded a lot less crazy after seeing fire shoot-ing from my own fingertips.

"Okay," I said slowly as if I was talking to a tod-dler, "what do you suppose I do to bring back my memory?"

"I'm glad you asked," she said and plopped her-self down happily on the couch and patted the cush-ion next to her for me to join her. "Do you want to do this the easy way or the hard way," she said and rolled her shoulders like Tina Turner. Before I could make my decision, she interjected, "the hard way is gonna be a lot faster than the easy way."

Feeling like she just made the decision for me I shrugged my shoulders, "Let's do it the hard way then". She clapped her hands giddily, way to giddy for something that she deemed the hard way. She then held her hand out towards a bookcase that was lining her wall. Her hand was still about two feet away from the bookcase, when a book floated towards her outstretched palm.

My eyes grew wide, I'd seen some strange shit in my day, but this took the cake. She noticed my expression and giggled a little "What the hell are you?" I asked.

"Says the guy who torched my sink with his bare hands," she quipped. "I'm a witch silly," she said like she was explaining something to a four-year-old. She opened the book, a dense ancient looking tome encased in black leather with gold symbols on it.

"And what's that floaty book thing?" This time she laughed a loud and throaty laugh, throwing her head back and making the cascade of locs ripple and undulate like a million tiny ribbons. Her laugh combined with the beautiful sight that she was made me want to kiss her right then and there, but I didn't. I just looked into her dark brown eyes as they crinkled with mirth and wetness. She wiped her eyes with her hands and I caught sight of a light patch of skin on the back of her hand. The creamy buttermilk color contrasted against the tawny brown of the rest of her skin that reminded me of wet sand on the beach. Seeing my eyes on her hand she quickly tucked it under her right leg.

"It's vitiligo, okay," she said in a huff. I nodded my head and she went to open the book. I touched her hand before she could and lifted my shirt to show her my ruined left side. The left side of my torso was a mess of burn scars and skin grafts. It earned me a Purple Heart but made me self-conscious about going to the beach. I wanted her to know I understood how something others might seem an imperfection might make you want to hide.

She reached out and touched my scars ever so lightly. I felt her fingertips glide over the rough terrain of the scars feather light. Wordlessly she lifted up her long maxi skirt and I got more excited than I should have. Her legs were lithe, muscular, and contained a multitude of those buttermilk patches creating a map to a destination that I vowed to myself that I would visit before I took my last breath.

"You're beautiful," I said.

My voice hitched, and my manhood strained against the stiff fabric of my chinos, a traitor to the perilous situation I seemed to be in. Here I was shooting fire from my fingers and my dick was trying to take over my thought process. I shook my head to try and make way for rational thought, but it was difficult with her still standing there with her skirt hoisted around her creamy thighs. I touched her hand again and she dropped the fabric of her skirt.

"The hard way?" I asked bringing both of our attention back to the problem at hand.

She cleared her throat and walked over to the fridge. When she came back to where I was seated she had two Coronas in her hands. She pressed one into my open hand.

"Sorry I'm all out of limes."

FEARLESS

BY

BALOGUN OJETADE

Keita Bojang, great Mansakeh of the King-
dom of Mali, sat before Jubeh, the Royal Diviner.
The old, blind man had been summoned to the palace to consult the oracle on the recent birth of his
son, Anjai...and on the passing of Anjai's mother,
Maala.

Anjai stared into Jubeh's sightless eyes as the
old man placed the boy's tiny, right foot into a bowl
of warm sand. Anjai cooed and giggled as the sand
tickled his plump, little toes.
Jubeh grabbed a fistful of the sand and tossed it
onto the floor. He rocked back and forth as the Ali-
faa Faloloo – the ancestors – spoke to him. Great
King Keita cradled Anjai in his arms and awaited
instructions from the spirits.

Jubeh's rocking stopped. His head fell
against his shoulder and his chest heaved as he took
a deep breath.

"Anjai is to exceed, in skill and wits, all the children of this great nation, past and present."

Mansakeh Keita smiled and then kissed Anjai on the forehead.

"However," Jubeh sighed. "He will bring you much heartache, as he will leave this world long before you."

The Mansakeh's jaw fell slack. "What?! How?"

"He will be killed by an animal," Jubeh replied. "Either an ape, a crocodile, or a dog. The ancestors will not say, specifically, which."

"What can we do to prevent this?" Mansakeh Keita asked, wiping tears from his cheeks.

"Nothing, Great One," Jubeh replied. "The ancestors have decreed it so."

"I am Keita Bojang," the Mansakeh spat. "Mansakeh of Mali, the greatest nation in all Ki-Khanga. There is *nothing* that I cannot do!"

"Great One, the ancestors have spoken; we..."

"*I* have spoken!" Mansakeh Keita shouted as he sprang to his feet.

Anjai kicked his feet and giggled.

"What the ancestors have revealed is a warning; nothing more," the Mansakeh said. "I will ensure my son's safety and he *will* rule Mali upon my passing."

"Yes, Great One," Jubeh sighed.

The great king sauntered out of his chamber and stumbled into the courtyard, where he rocked Anjai into a deep and peaceful sleep.

*　*　*

Anjai whirled, kicking up clouds of red dirt as he rent the air with his broadsword. He drew a figure-eight pattern in the air with the razor-sharp steel and then thrust the sword into the stiff, leather scabbard that hung from his belt.

"Your technique is superb," a familiar voice bellowed.

"Thank you, father," Anjai said, turning toward the Mansakeh. "Perhaps, one day soon, I will be blessed to use what I have learned over all these years on the battlefield, in service to the great Mansakeh Keita."

The Mansakeh hung his head. "Son, you *will* leave this compound one day. Please, be patient."

"But, I am terribly lonely, father," Anjai sighed. "I live half a day's ride from Timbuktu...from *you*; and there is not another living human soul anywhere near here."
"You have your housekeeper and your personal guard," Mansakeh Keita said. "And I visit as often as I can."

"Uli and Asuru are not big on conversation, father," Anjai said. "And this is your first visit in two moon cycles."

"Shall I throw a celebration in your honor, then?" the Mansakeh asked. "I can bring the best drummers and dancers and the most beautiful women in all Timbuktu, including that young woman who had you so smitten at your last celebration – the daughter of the Alikaalah of Diari – what is her name..."

"Akinah," Anjai replied.

"Akinah! That's it! I can invite her."

"No, father," Anjai said, shaking his head. "My desires are less...complex."

"What, then?" the Mansakeh asked.

"I want a puppy," Anjai answered.

Mansakeh Keita's brow furrowed and the corners of his mouth curled downward. "No, son; no puppies...*ever!*"

"Why not?" Anjai asked. "A friendly puppy..."

"Will become a *dog*," the Mansakeh spat. "And a dog may be the death of you!"

Anjai's heart raced. Sweat ran down his forehead and dripped from the tip of his nose, leaving tiny pools in the sand between his feet. "The death of me? How so?"

The Mansakeh paced back and forth, rubbing his temple with the tips of his fingers. He squeezed his eyes shut, as if to prevent from seeing the painful truth.

"When you were born, the Royal Diviner told me that you would meet your fate through an encounter with an ape, a crocodile, or a *dog*."

"Then, it is possible that a dog will not be the culprit?" Anjai asked.

"It is possible," Mansakeh Keita answered.

"Then, I am willing to take that chance," Anjai said. "If I raise it with love and kindness, would it dare harm me?"

"You have a point," the Mansakeh said, rubbing his smooth, ebon chin. "Alright, then, I will send forth my wisest advisors to find the friendliest, most intelligent newborn puppy in all Mali!"

Anjai's heart soared the moment he laid eyes upon the playful, stark-white Azawakh pup that the Wise Ones had chosen for him. "He is beautiful, father! I know we will become the closest of friends.

"What will you call him, son?" the Mansakeh asked.

"His name is...'Fatinga'," Anjai replied.

"Fearless," Mansakeh Keita said, with a nod. "That is a good name."

Mansakeh Keita placed a hand upon his son's sinewy shoulder.

"Son, while the Wise Ones searched high and low for your pup, they heard that the Alikaalah of Diari seeks a young man to wed his daughter. The Alikaalah is a dear friend and has led Diari well on my behalf. It would please me if you married Akinah."

"When will you arrange the marriage, father?" Anjai inquired.

"It is not that simple," the Mansakeh replied. "The Alikaalah of Diari loves tests of strength, bravery and wits; thus, he has put forth a challenge."

"Which is?" Anjai asked, raising an eyebrow.

"The first to scale the wall of the Alikaalah's palace and climb through his daughter's window – which is on the uppermost floor – wins her hand in marriage," the Mansakeh replied.

"How high is this wall, father?"

"Seventy cubits," the Mansakeh replied. "One hundred and five feet."

"Has anyone tried such a treacherous climb?" Anjai asked.

"Many," the Mansakeh answered. "They all fell to their deaths. Does that frighten you, son?"

"No, father," Anjai replied. "Not one bit."

"*That's* my boy," the Mansakeh said, beaming. "The Bojang bloodline is notorious for exceptional bravery!"

"It is not bravery that makes me so assured father," Anjai said. "It is knowing that I will die by ape, dog or crocodile...*not* by a fall."

"Ha!" The Mansakeh bellowed. "Sometimes, a fox's head serves a warrior better than a lion's heart."

* * *

The carriage ride to Diari was the happiest moment of Anjai's life. He was finally free of the confines of his compound. He thrust his head out of the window of his carriage, relishing the kiss of the desert breeze upon his face. His camels raced across the network of sand roads, spurred on by the expert handling of Anjai's bodyguard, Asuru.

After a day-and-a-half ride, Anjai arrived in the bustling town of Diari – the *City of Gold* – the location of the largest gold mine in all the lands of Ki-Khanga. The palace of the Alikaalah was constructed entirely of gold. Its interior and exterior walls, floors, doors and ramparts – all gold.

Anjai's carriage was met by Idris Ul-Arbah, Chief of the Palace Guard, as it approached the palace. "How may we help you, kind sir?"

"I am Anjai, son of Mansakeh Keita Bojang," Anjai replied. "And I have come to win the hand of the Alikaalah's daughter."

Idris dropped to one knee. "Welcome, Your Highness. Will you need accommodations for the night?"

"No," Anjai replied, stepping down from his carriage. "I will scale the wall after a brief stretch."

"As you wish," Idris said, rising to his feet. The Chief of the Palace Guard turned and sauntered back through the palace gates.

Anjai bent forward and touched the ground with his palms, stretching the muscles in his back and legs. He held the position for a few minutes and then stood bolt upright. "I am ready, now."

Asuru nodded.

Anjai sprinted toward the eastern wall of the palace – his father's informants had told him that Akinah's chamber was on that side – which was dotted, from-top-to-bottom, with golden spikes, each as thick around as a man's wrist and protruding two feet out of the wall. He exploded upward, thrusting his arms above his head. He grabbed one of the spikes with both hands and pulled himself up until his feet rested firmly on a spike beneath him. He exploded upward again and again, grabbing the spikes over his head and pulling himself ever closer to Akinah's window.

Finally, he reached it. He swung his legs toward the open window and tumbled inside. Anjai landed with a dull thud as his buttocks struck the golden floor.

He fought off the pain and pulled himself to his feet. Sitting on a bed of plush, pastel-colored pillows was Akinah, who was even more beautiful than Anjai remembered.

"I am Anjai," he began. "Son of Mansakeh Keita Bojang..."

"I know who you are," Akinah giggled. "Cease with the formalities; we are to be married in less than a fortnight. Soon, I will be scolding you for passing gas in our sleeping chamber. How informal can you be?"

"Gods, you are so beautiful," Anjai said, taking a seat beside her.

"More importantly, I am highly intelligent, skilled in business and spent eight years in Fez, training under the greatest wizards to ever traverse the sands of Ki-Khanga," Akinah said.

"Does my complimenting you on your beauty offend you?" Anjai inquired.

"No," Akinah replied. You merely speak truth. However, if you are going to shower me with compliments, please be fully accurate in your descriptions."

Anjai laughed. For the first time since he left his compound, he looked forward to returning home, for he would return with a magnificent friend and partner to share it with.

* * *

Akinah awakened with a start. A frightening din came from the kitchen below. She recognized the noise as the snarls of an angry canine. Something had Fatinga quite vexed.

Akinah now loved the dog – and he, her – but when Anjai first told her of the ancestors' decree on how her husband would die, she begged Anjai to kill the Azawakh. She was now happy that he refused, for the dog had proven time and again to be a loyal and protective companion to the couple.

Akinah gently shook her husband's broad shoulders, awakening him.

"What is it, my love?" Anjai asked, rubbing his eyes.

"It is Fatinga," Akinah whispered. "He is growling at something in the kitchen."

Anjai sprang from the bed and grabbed a pair of cotton trousers. "I hear him!"
Akinah stood and threw on her silk robe.

"If I ask you to stay here, will you oblige?" Anjai asked, as he snatched his broadsword its ivory stand.

Akinah pursed her lips and raised an eyebrow in reply.

"I thought not," Anjai said with a shrug. "Let's go!"

Anjai darted down the stairs. Akinah followed closely behind him. They sprinted toward the kitchen. Fatinga stood defiantly, baring his teeth and snarling at a half dozen squat, husky figures, which lurked in the shadows.

"Show yourselves!" Anjai demanded as he inched closer to the kitchen.

The figures lumbered out of the shadows. They were chimpanzees, but their eyes revealed an intelligence and a brutality possessed only by man. All except one were black as pitch, with wrinkled, pink faces, twisted into harsh scowls. At the head of the apes stood one who was slightly taller than its brethren and of a sandy complexion. The sand-hued chimp raised its right arm high. Dangling from its fingers was the severed head of Anjai's bodyguard, Asuru.

"Belong you, him does?" the sand-colored creature snickered in the native, human Ki-Khanga tongue.

"He was my bodyguard, monster!" Anjai spat.

"Him not guard you body too good," the chimpanzee said.

A shrill laughter erupted from the other chimps.

"Leave now, ape and we will let you live," Anjai said.

"We leave, you mate come with," the leader ape said. "She Gold King baby; we trade she with Gold King for lot gold; lot food."

"No," Anjai said.

"Wokay," the sand-hued ape said with a shrug. "We kill and take mate, then."

The chimpanzees charged forward. Fatinga leapt toward one, sinking his fangs into the ape's neck as he ripped at the creature's belly with his rear paws. The ape let loose a hissing gurgle as blood erupted from its neck and its entrails spilled onto the floor.

Anjai rolled forward, delivering a powerful thrust as his momentum brought him to a kneeling position. His sword sank into the chest of a charging chimpanzee. The creature shuddered and then slid off the blade, collapsing, with a loud thud, onto its back.

Akinah waved her hands in wide circles in front of her, as if she was scrubbing the floor with her palms. A huge hole opened beneath the feet of a pair of chimpanzees that sprinted toward her. The apes plummeted into the deep hole. A moment later, the cavity closed over them, muffling their cries of terror.

The sand-colored ape and the surviving pitch-black ape spun on their heels and dived out of an open kitchen window. Their cries pierced the night calm as they scurried off into the shadows of the desert oasis.

"Is everyone alright?" Anjai asked, his eyes darting from Akinah to Fatinga.

"I'm fine, love," Akinah replied.

Fatinga replied with a throaty bark.

"At least we know that it won't be any ape that is the death of you," Akinah said.

"They can always return," Anjai said.

"And we will fill ape-heaven with them all," Akinah half-quipped.

"Get some rest, you two," Anjai said. "Tomorrow morning, we burn these foul creatures and bury Asuru."

* * *

The day was exceptionally beautiful. Anjai was invigorated by the gentle breeze, which caressed and cooled him as he breast-stroked in the warm waters of the Sati-Baa River.

Akinah gathered moist sand from the shore in a calabash. She poured the sand onto the ground and sculpted it into little figurines. Fatinga paced back-and-forth along the shoreline as he kept a watchful eye on Anjai. The dog unleashed a high-pitched howl.

Akinah looked up from her sculptures and spotted the head of a large crocodile break the surface of the water just a few yards from her unsuspecting husband. Fatinga howled again.

"Anjai," Akinah shouted, pointing at the massive crocodile. "Behind you!"

Anjai peered over his shoulder. He screamed in terror and began to swim furiously. The crocodile was hot on his fluttering heels.

Akinah glanced at her sand sculptures. They had fused together, forming themselves into the perfect likeness of a crocodile. The sorceress stomped the tip of the sand crocodile's tail. A moment later, the real crocodile hissed and thrashed in agony. The water around the crocodile became a deep crimson. With a swipe of the back of her hand, Akinah knocked off a piece of the sand sculpture's jaw. The real crocodile thrashed violently in the water as its lower jaw disjointed and then fell from the crocodile's head. The wedge-shaped mass of flesh, bone and teeth floated up-shore as the crocodile sank beneath the surface of the water.

Anjai swam to shore. He scampered out of the water and then sprinted into his wife's open arms. "You saved me!" He planted brisk kisses upon his wife's forehead and cheeks. He then knelt next to Fatinga and rubbed his neck. "You did well, little brother. Thank you!" Fatinga wagged his tail.

"As long as you have Fatinga and me around, no harm will befall you," Akinah said. "You will live to see your grandchildren grow old. We should tell your father about..."

A sound, like distant thunder, rent the air.

"Someone approaches," Anjai said, pointing toward a fast approaching mass in the distance.

A woman on camelback galloped toward them. Her leathery skin was as dark as the smooth, mahogany saddle upon which she sat.

"Your Highness," the woman called, bringing the camel to a stop a yard from them.

Akinah recognized the woman as Nura, her father's Emissary. "Yes?"

"Your mother has fallen very ill," Nura replied. "She asks for you; your father has commanded that I escort your carriage to Diari at once. I have already alerted your driver. He and your housekeeper are packing your travel bag as we speak."

"I will ride with you," Anjai said.

"No, my love," Akinah said. "There is an old woman along the way who possesses a deep knowledge of healing herbs. I will hire her services, see that my mother is well-cared for and return home in less than half a fortnight.

"Fine," Anjai said. "When you return, I would like to begin laying the foundation for those grandchildren whom I will usher into old age."

Akinah blushed as she jogged toward their compound. "Why wait? Escort me back to the compound and let's lay that foundation before I depart."

"As you command," Anjai said, chasing her.

Fatinga trotted behind his masters, gleefully wagging his tail.

*   *   *

Anjai awoke to the smell of fresh horned melon and yogurt with a hint of vanilla. Uli had prepared his favorite breakfast. He darted out of bed, threw on a pair of loose-fitting, linen trousers and a waist-length tunic and then darted down the stairs, not stopping until he reached the dining room.

"I saama," Uli said in greeting. *"Good morning."*

Anjai returned the greeting – "I saama."

The elderly woman bent slightly at the waist in salutation and then left Anjai to enjoy his meal.

Anjai devoured the food, gulped down two cups of water and then jogged out the door. Fatinga burst out the door behind him.

"How far shall we run, Fatinga?" Anjai asked, patting the dog's head. "Two miles?"

Fatinga barked in approval.

"Two miles it is, then," Anjai said.

Man and dog trotted along the sand and gravel road leading out of the compound.

After a short while, Fatinga stopped running. He stared up at the palm trees that lined the trail. A low growl rose from his gut.

Anjai knelt beside Fatinga. "What is it, little brother?"

From out of the trees descended a score of pitch-hued chimpanzees. The apes landed in a series of dull thuds, kicking up clouds of sand and red dirt as each hit the ground. When the dust cleared, an army of apes stood before Anjai. Standing a yard ahead of the chimpanzees was their sand-colored leader.

"'Member we Mkeko?" The leader of the apes asked. "We Mkeko 'member you. You kill we Mkeko; now, Mkeko return favor!"

The apes lurched forward in unison.

"Fatinga, run!" Anjai commanded, as he dashed off the trail.

Anjai exploded into a full sprint, with Fatinga running close behind him. The Mkeko gave chase, some trotting across the sand and dirt, others swinging and leaping through the trees. Anjai ran on and on; out of his compound; across the oasis upon which his home was built...and into a pool of quicksand. Anjai tried to swim out of it, but the grainy liquid was too thick. Within moments, only his torso was visible above the surface. Fatinga barked at Anjai, as if to scold him for putting himself into such a dangerous predicament. Soft footsteps approached. Fatinga whirled toward the sound. The sand-colored chimpanzee was coming. Fatinga snarled viciously. The ape stopped a few yards from the dog and pointed at Anjai, who had now sunk to his chest.

"You run right where we Mkeko want, silly man. Now, we Mkeko wait for Gold-King baby come home; we Mkeko take daughter; trade for lot gold; lot food. Bye-bye, silly man."

The sand-hued chimpanzee turned and walked back toward the army of Mkeko, which awaited him in the distance.

"Fatinga," Anjai called. "Run back to the compound. When Uli sees you arrive without me, she will come looking."

Fatinga did not budge. He stood his ground, growling to keep the surrounding Mkeko at bay.

Anjai sank farther. Sand rushed into the top of his tunic. "Fatinga, hurry!"

The dog refused to leave its master alone and unprotected. It fearlessly stood its ground.
Sand slapped Anjai in the chin.

"Fatinga...please."

Fatinga did not budge.

As Anjai sank completely beneath the surface of the quicksand, he realized that the ancestors, indeed, spoke truth. He had met his fate through a dog. A protective, loyal and fearless one.

WRATH

BY

KYOKO M

Being Jordan Amador's angelic bodyguard against a horde of bloodthirsty demons was a lot of things, but certainly not boring.

I checked my watch for the fortieth time in the last twenty minutes. Jordan usually got off at eight o'clock. Things had been quiet for over two weeks now, which was rare for a Seer's lifestyle. She encountered ghosts with unfinished business a few times a month and that kept the both of us busy. Earlier, she had convinced me to meet her at the bus stop a couple streets over instead of in front of the Sweet Spot.

"So would you mind waiting for me at the bus stop instead of out here?" she had asked, sweeping her shoulder-length black hair up into its usual high ponytail.

I frowned. "Why? Doesn't it kind of defeat the purpose of the whole 'temporary bodyguard' thing?"

"It's been quiet for a while now, Michael. Come on. Ganking an archdemon isn't enough to prove I can take care of myself?"

I glanced between her and the store front. A couple of her waitress friends who were watching us through the window scattered as soon as I looked over. Then it clicked.

"They think I'm your boyfriend, huh?"

Jordan got really interested in her shoes all of the sudden. "Yeah. They do."

I shook my head. She was an anointed soul charged with helping the dead find peace and yet she still cared what her coworkers thought of our relationship. I couldn't decide if it was cute, frustrating, or hilarious. Possibly all three.

Then again, I could see how her coworkers would get confused when a six-foot-tall, dark-haired, green-eyed "underwear model" (which I overheard one of them dub me last week) dropped Jordan off at work on a frequent basis. I decided to be lenient for once.

"Fine. We'll give it a test run today. If you survive, I'll take it into consideration."

She shot me a scowl. "Gee, thanks, almighty Michael. I am humbled that you considered the request of a lowly human."

I grinned. "You're welcome, my humble servant."

She rolled her eyes and swatted my arm before turning to head into the restaurant. "Later, pretty boy."

"Stay out of trouble." I called, and then headed back towards the bus stop.

That had been eight hours ago. Getting off a shift late wasn't unusual for a waitress, but most times it was by only five or ten minutes. My instincts needled at me that something was off.

Sighing, I fished out my cell phone and called her, tapping my foot. "Come on, Amador, pick up."

Several rings. A click. Voicemail message. Ugh. I hung up and stuffed my hands in my pockets. It was a short walk through the heavily trafficked area on this side of Albany, New York, but it was during one of the busier times of the day. Nighttime in the city meant chatty couples walking through holding hands, teenagers hollering and chasing each other down the street, and music pouring out from the clubs already packed to the rafters with twenty-somethings.

Two stop lights, one near-death experience courtesy of a speeding cab, and one step in some gum later, and I reached the glowing red sign to the Sweet Spot. The Southern cuisine eatery was busy. As much as Northerners made fun of the South in sitcoms and stand up shows, they sure did like the food.

I pushed the door open and smiled at Beth, the head hostess. "Hey, you."

"Michael." The short blonde grinned. "Good to see you, as always."

"Is Jordan still in the back?"

A slight frown marred her brow. "No, honey. She left about ten minutes ago."

I froze. "Left how? She was supposed to meet me at the bus stop."

"She went out back to take out the trash and I just assumed she went home after. Why? Something wrong?"

A cold lump settled in my stomach. Something wasn't adding up. Jordan wasn't the type to disappear without texting me. I didn't want to concern her friends so I kept my expression pleasant. "Nah, she probably just wandered off to window shop. I'll catch up with her. Thanks, Beth."

"No problem, sweets."

I made a point to leave the restaurant in a casual manner, but once I was out of sight, I hurried around the block to the back of the building. The Sweet Spot was part of an entertainment district in this section of Albany. There were narrow alleys between the establishments and the streets ran parallel to the store fronts.

The Sweet Spot's back alley looked like any other restaurant in Albany—lined by dumpsters and garbage cans. The concrete was littered with fallen bits of food. A couple of mangy cats fought over fish bones. The entire area stank to high heaven. I called Jordan's phone again and prayed that my instincts were wrong.

The raucous chorus to Right Said Fred's "I'm Too Sexy" echoed behind me.

I turned towards one of the dumpsters and lifted the entire thing with one hand. Her phone lay cracked and forlorn underneath it.

Shit.

I tucked her phone in my pocket, forcing myself to calm down. Think. What was my next move? Calling the cops would be ill-advised. They'd take forever, and even if they found her, there was no telling how many innocent officers could die trying to save her. I knew angels in the police department, but they couldn't drop everything for me. Better check for evidence.

Jordan had basic self-defense skills and moderate experience fighting demons, so I guessed it would have taken more than one of them to subdue her. The lack of blood implied that they didn't hurt her on the spot, so that ruled out an assassination attempt. Two weeks ago, Jordan and I had foiled a plot by the archdemon Belial and sent him back to Hell. I bargained with the heavenly Father to remain on earth at her side in case Belial wanted retaliation. Up until today, there were no attempts on her life. Stupidly, I'd let my guard down and now she was gone.

The alley was wide, but blind. It led to a small road to the right. They would've parked the car there, jumped her and knocked her out, and then carried her to it. The assailants needed to haul ass to avoid anyone seeing an unconscious woman tied up and thrown into their trunk.

I dialed Gabriel's number. It rang a few times, but he picked up eventually.

"Michael. How are you this fine evening?"

"Jordan's in trouble."

My brother's voice hardened into granite. Not surprising. He'd known Jordan longer than I had and was fiercely fond of her as well. "What happened?"

"I think someone made off with her after her shift at the restaurant. I'm there now. I need you to find the closest demon's nest to here. I'll give you the address."

"Alright, go."

After I told him, I paced back and forth as I waited, my mind whirring with theories. The average demon never kept the same nest location. They switched every couple of weeks because they knew angels tracked them. The places they used were always abandoned, foreclosed, or in rough neighborhoods thick with crime. Most demons were under orders to keep tabs on one another and dispense orders from any of the five Princes of Hell. The ones who kidnapped Jordan were probably members of the local gang of losers.

"One of our sentries says there is an old

house outside the city where they take their victims. This particular establishment is akin to..."

"Akin to what, Gabe?"

He exhaled. "...a slaughterhouse. The angels with the police department have been trying to gather evidence, but all they have is missing people and no traces of the murders."

Slaughterhouse. Images of Jordan strung up and split open flickered through my mind.

"Text me the address."

"Michael—"

"Text. Me. The. Address."

"...yes, brother."

I hung up and waited, trying to distract myself with positive thoughts. Jordan wasn't some damsel in distress. She was smart, tough, stubborn, and a crack shot. If she'd been carrying when the demons came for her, I might not have been on this rescue mission.

My phone buzzed with a text message a second later that had the address. Time to go.

Under any other circumstance, I'd take a cab, but Jordan was in the company of murderers, which gave me a valid excuse to bend the rules.

I summoned my spiritual energy from deep within. Coolness billowed through my limbs and filled them with supernatural powers. Once it thrummed through my veins, I opened my eyes and concentrated on the most direct route from here. I bounced on my heels once, twice, thrice, and then released the clutch.

To the untrained eye, I'd seem like nothing more than a heavy breeze, but in reality, I was running so swiftly that not even the fastest shutter speed on a digital camera could see me. I darted between cars, around fire hydrants, on the outskirts of the crowded sidewalks between the restaurant and the demons' nest. Huge gusts of wind kicked up in my wake, scattering fallen bits of trash and scaring the hell out of several dogs. The distance from here to there was about eight miles. I made to the area in less than five minutes.

The house was at the bottom of a hill of long dead brown grass and surrounded by a high black iron fence. The exterior had been painted white at some point, but the wood on the outside was mildewed and splintered all to hell. It looked more grey than anything else, like one of those hideous places children made up ghost stories about.

The property was situated by itself for several acres, ensuring that no neighbors would ever hear the screams of their victims. I estimated Jordan had been with him for less than an hour, so it was likely they hadn't hurt her too much. If they had...God help them.

I pressed my back against the gate. Ivy leaves tickled the nape of my neck as I huddled there and sniffed the air twice. Faint scent of sulfur. Hellhounds. If they saw me, my chances of getting her back unharmed would be slim. Their barks could be heard for miles. I'd have to keep them quiet.

Gathering my legs beneath me, I leapt over the six-foot fence and landed on my knees in the cool grass. The front yard was about thirty feet from the porch. No hounds yet.

I stayed low and slunk towards the rear of the house, stepping lightly to muffle the crunch of the brown grass underfoot. I made it to the side of the house and flattened myself against the flaking paint on the walls. I peeked around the corner.

There were four hellhounds—each the size of

a full grown mountain lion and covered from head to toe in shaggy black fur. Two were lying on the wooden back porch, sleeping. The other two entertained themselves with the hollow shell of an Oldsmobile. One yanked off the driver's side door and tore into the upholstery as if it were nothing more than paper. Another raked its sharp claws down the rear passenger's side. The metal screamed under its nails. It yawned, revealing rows of long glistening yellow fangs that could rip through solid steel.

They hadn't smelled me yet. I was downwind, but they'd catch my scent if I made a move toward them. Then again, maybe that was what I wanted.

I slipped my seven-inch retractable Green Beret knife out of my back pocket and cut a thin line across my left palm. Warm blood dripped from it onto the grass. Low growls reached my ears. I checked around the corner again. All of them were awake and sniffing the air, their long ears flattened against their skulls. Nothing attracted hellhounds like fresh blood.

Quickly, I scattered a wide circle of blood droplets in the grass and then stood just outside of it. All four hounds came dashing around the corner, their red eyes like deadly firelight in the dark, and they pounced straight at me.

As soon as their bodies crossed the blood lines, a flash of red light shot upward and trapped them inside the circle. They smashed against an invisible force field and collapsed into a limp, whimpering doggy pile. I extended my bloody hand and spoke the Latin incantation to exorcise them. Black smoke poured out of their thick hides and then evaporated, shrinking them down to normal size. When the hellish energy dissipated, I was left with two pit bulls, a golden Labrador, and a beagle. They sat on their haunches and wagged their tails, confused but happy to see me.

I continued around the back of the house. It was a farmhouse with three steps leading to the porch with a rickety swing and a screen door. The windows were boarded up. No matter. I wouldn't be going in that way anyhow. Demons were smart enough not to do their dirty work above ground level.

The west side of the house had exactly what I had been hoping for—an old-fashioned storm cellar door. A heavy chain was wound around the rusty handles, but that didn't make a difference. No force on earth was going to stop me from getting her back.

I pressed my hand against the rotted wood and uncurled my spiritual energy enough to sense if there was anyone home. Then I felt it. Jordan's energy signature. She was here, and she was still alive. Relief spilled over me like cool spring water.

I straightened and held my arm up to the night sky. Grey clouds slid together over the moon and darkness gathered. The wind kicked my hair into my eyes. A low grumble of thunder answered my call. Lightning flashed and then my sword flew down into my hand. Its long, narrow blade glowed like silver fire in the dark, aching to be used.

A dark part of me chuckled at the thought of what the demons would do when they found out the archangel Michael had come for their captive. The sword itself would be enough to scare them shitless—it was akin to a saber, with a thin, slightly curved blade that was lightweight and easy to wield. The handle was pure silver with patterns beaten into it depicting the moment I had cut the side of Satan and assured our victory.

Male voices reached my ears as I sliced through the chains holding the cellar doors shut.

"Hey, did you hear thunder just now?"

"No. All I hear is your gums flapping. Now hold her still. I can't do anything with her wiggling around like she is."

Don't charge in, I reminded myself as the last of the chains fell aside. *You might get her killed. Stay smart.*

The door's old hinges creaked just a bit as I lifted it enough to see into the basement. The stench of dust and rot flooded into my nostrils. The basement was dimly lit with a few naked bulbs so my eyes had to adjust. Concrete floors. Mold. Cobwebs. The room was L-shaped, with the stairs on the left and the main room towards the right. Work tables had been pushed against the far wall, along with discarded furniture. Bloody instruments crowded nearly every available surface.

There were two demons standing in front of Jordan—one chunky blond with curly hair and the other thin with black buzzcut hair. They were both in jeans and wifebeaters despite the chill of the basement air. The blond had a fresh burn scar along the left side of his neck that I knew was the result of holy water. The dark-haired demon's forearms were stained from several cuts. The skin below his left eye puffed like he'd been punched.

Jordan hung from her wrists, swinging gently as the curly haired demon came up behind her. Her eyes were half-lidded as if she'd been tired out from fighting. Dried blood crusted on her forehead, probably from where they'd knocked her out. The entire right side of her throat shone dark red with blood. Some of it had dripped onto her white dress shirt. The bottom of her knee-length black skirt was torn. Her fingernails had something brownish underneath them. She hadn't been an easy captive. Good girl.

The blond demon's hands gripped her waist. Jordan thrashed like a landed shark. Her brown eyes opened completely and she kicked the dark-haired demon right in the nose. His head snapped back, but he didn't cry out as blood splattered down the front of his face.

Buzzcut wiped the blood off his chin and spat out a mouthful. He laughed and twirled the butcher knife in his hand. Demons were built to take punishment like that a thousand times over. Jordan knew that; I assumed she'd done it just to spite them.

"Man, she's a live one," the dark-haired demon said. "She's still fighting."

"I'll dope her with something in a minute. Hurry up. That first taste wasn't enough. I'm hungry."

Jordan tried to say something through her gag. Buzzcut held the knife under her chin and growled, "You scream and I'll slit your throat."

He pulled the filthy rag down from her lips. She took a couple of breaths and then gave him a death glare. "Last chance, knuckleheads. Let me go or you're both dead."

Curly laughed. "God, I love her. The other Seers weren't nearly this much fun. We've got you all to ourselves and you're still convinced you can win."

"Not *can*, you ass-clown. Will."

"Oh yeah?" Buzzcut sneered. "What makes you so sure of that?"

"Because there's an archangel standing behind you."

Buzzcut didn't get out another word. I ran him through with one stroke. The tip burst through his chest cavity and he choked on his last breath, stricken.

Curly screamed as his friend hit the floor, his eyes so wide they looked like China plates with olive pits in the middle. He held an eight-inch bayonet knife beneath Jordan's ribs, using her as a human shield.

"Take one step closer and she's dead!" he shrieked.

"Get...your hands...*off*...my friend," I said through clenched teeth.

"Drop the sword. I swear I'll spear the little bitch like a roasted pig if you don't." To emphasize his point, he jabbed the blade into her side. She jerked in her restraints and dark red blossomed outward like a morbid rose pattern in her blouse.

My fingers tightened around the hilt. I glanced at Jordan. "Close your eyes."

"What?"

"I don't want you to see this."

She gave me a searching look and then did as I asked.

"Last warning. Back away from her."

"And I told you to—AAAAGH!"

I sliced his right arm off at the shoulder. The bayonet and his arm hit the floor with a sickening thud. Blood sprayed all three of us. Curly, still screaming, stumbled away from Jordan. I took a stance in front of her.

"You son of a bitch!" the demon spat as he fumbled for the knife still clasped in his dismembered hand. "I'll kill you!"

He ran at me with the weapon aloft, aiming for my head. I caught his wrist on the downward stroke and shoved the sword through the space above his collarbone. He jerked forward and twitched, staring at me from inches away. Fear filled those beady eyes, followed by panic. Blood oozed from the wound, joining the widening puddle made by his severed arm.

A nasty chuckle escaped my lips. "Congratulations, demon. You have finally managed to piss me off."

I tightened my grip on his wrist and broke it in one swift movement. He cried out again. I savored the sound. I kicked his left kneecap and he collapsed in front of me. I left the sword where it pierced him instead of going for the killing blow. He broke into violent shudders. More blood welled from between his lips and spilled down his front.

"You must have heard by now what happened with Belial. He set his sights on this woman and thought he could just take what he wanted from her. He was sorely mistaken, as you are right now."

I grabbed a handful of his hair and jerked his head back so he'd have to look up at me. "She restored my life. Without her, I'd be walking the earth lost and alone. You must understand how it makes me feel that you've got her strung up like some bovine carcass."

"D-Didn't know...you were...protecting her..." the demon stammered in between wet gulping breaths. "Just thought she was...alone..."

"But that's what you do, isn't it?" I said, casually twisting the blade a bit just to watch him cringe. "You stalk and you feast on those that you think are your prey without considering the consequences."

I ripped my sword out of his chest and then kicked him in the sternum. He fell onto his back. I jammed the tip of the blade through his left hand, pinning it to the floor. He bucked upward with convulsions and a whimper crawled out of his throat.

"P-Please just k-kill me. I'll never t-touch another Seer again. I s-swear!"

"Why should I show you mercy? You weren't going to do the same. Maybe I should just cut loose. No one will find you here. I could lay into you for hours. Make you a tourniquet for that arm and slice you open. See what makes you tick. Pull your soul out of that fat dump of a body and toy with it until I've had my fill. Does that sound fun to you, demon?"

I shoved the sword an inch deeper into the punctured mess in his hand and he yowled like a beast with its leg in a bear trap.

Then Jordan spoke from behind me.

"Michael, please."

Just those two words were like a bucket of ice water dumped over my head. I realized what I'd been doing. Her safety was far more important than my desire for revenge. Still, I couldn't let this slimy bastard think I'd gone soft.

"Take this message to your people, you obsequious little worm," I murmured. "Anyone who lays a hand on Jordan Amador will have to answer to me. Now do me a favor and *go to hell.*"

I removed my sword from his hand and then decapitated him. His severed head tumbled across the floor like a wayward bowling ball. Good riddance.

I set my sword aside, found a stool in the

corner, and climbed up in front of Jordan. Her handcuffs were attached to a huge meat hook bolted into the ceiling. I lifted her off of it with great care, unsure if she had the strength to stand. As soon as her arms were free, she looped them around my shoulders and pressed her face against my neck. She was trembling, but not crying. I sank to the floor and cradled her in my lap, breathing out the last of my anger now that she was safe.

"'M sorry," she mumbled in a small voice. "I'm so sorry, Michael."

I snorted. "What the hell do you have to apologize for? You got kidnapped. Pretty sure that's not your fault."

She shook her head, her words partially muffled as she pressed her face against my shirt. "Should've been stronger. I could've gotten you killed."

"By Heckle and Jeckle here? Not likely."

A shaky laugh rattled through her. She slid her fingers into the hairs along the nape of my neck and hugged me tighter. I knew from experience she didn't want me to see her face because she knew she was only seconds away from breaking down. No one would ever accuse Jordan Amador of being a crybaby, not if she could help it. It was a ridiculous notion at best, but I indulged her anyway.

"Thank you."

"Just doing my job. But you're welcome."

I smoothed the sweaty hairs away from her forehead enough to kiss it. She didn't move away. We stayed there for a while without speaking, just clinging to each other until we felt strong enough to separate.

Thankfully, aside from some bruises and the wound on her neck, she wasn't badly hurt. I broke her out of the cuffs and healed her before setting about to clean up our mess.

The demons had a huge compost heap in the backyard for disposing the unsavory bits of their victims, complete with copious amounts of lye. I dumped the bodies and then spread a liberal amount of lye on the corpses. Jordan didn't say anything, but she had no trouble helping me haul the bodies. She had seen her share of the dead, enough to last her a lifetime, I was sure.

I ended up gathering our bloodstained shirts together in a metal garbage pail and burning them. Nothing I knew of could get that much blood out. We didn't know if more demons would show up so there wasn't enough time to clean up in the bathroom upstairs. I found Jordan's duster balled up in the corner of the basement. Thankfully, it hid the residual stains on her upper body.

We caught a cab back to her apartment. She didn't eat anything for dinner, and I wasn't surprised. Instead, she slipped into the bathroom and took a long shower. I called Gabriel to let him know the matter had been resolved. He promised to drop by and see her in the morning.

Her bedroom door opened. I glanced over. She stood there with damp unkempt hair and oversized white Daffy Duck t-shirt. I couldn't identify the warm feeling blossoming inside my chest. It was probably for the best.

"Feeling any better?" I asked as I stood up from the couch.

She shrugged. "As good as I'm going to feel right now."

I nodded towards the rumpled covers on her bed. "Get some rest."

I turned to walk away, but then she caught

the hem of my shirt. I turned again. She immediately let go and stared at her bare feet.

"I know it's a lot to ask, but would you..."

I smiled. "Yeah."

She walked back into the bedroom. I shut the door and kicked off my shoes and socks. Jordan crawled onto the mattress and curled up on the left side. I settled down on the right. She pulled the covers up over her shoulders. I lay on my back, staring at the ceiling fan blades whirling above us.

I couldn't tell how long I'd been lying there, but sometime later the mattress moved next to me. I cracked open an eyelid to check on Jordan. She was curled up in the fetal position and shivering despite still being under the covers. *Shit.*

I scooted closer and touched her shoulder. She flinched, but didn't wake up. She was a heavy sleeper, after all.

I stroked the length of her arm for a moment or two. Gradually, the shaking slowed. After a minute, it stopped altogether. Her lithe body uncurled a little and the tension in her limbs vanished. There was still a lot I didn't know about this girl.

Once I was sure she was okay, I grabbed an extra pillow from the closet. I got back in bed, wedged it between our lower bodies, and then wrapped an arm around her waist. As soon as she felt my presence, she snuggled her back against my chest without ever waking. I had figured as much. She'd been in a long term relationship before she met me, and some habits never wore off. It wasn't until the next morning that I realized something startling.

I had never slept better.

EMBERS

BY

M. HAYNES

*Fire is everywhere. I open my eyes and it's
all I can see. Of course, it doesn't take long for me
to realize I have got to get out of here, so I jump
out of my bed and to wake up Paul and Tevin and
try to get them out too, but they're not there. I hope
to the Mystics that they got out already, but before
I can think any further a piece of the ceiling falls
down and I run out of our room.*

*The smoke gets thicker in the hallway; it's
like the whole building is on fire. I cough and
cough some more and try to run for the door. I
pass by the hallway to the girls' rooms, the cafete-
ria, even the spot where Mariah dared me to write
on the wall, all burning up. It's getting hot, even
for me, so when I get to the end of the main hallway I know I've got to hurry. Left turn, then a
quick right, and I can see the big trophy case with
the other kids' awards by the front door. Only*

*they're both on fire. I can't go back the way I came,
so I still run for it. I reach out to the burning door
and...some kind of way the fires disappear. Just
gone. I'm not gonna complain so I grab the handle
before the fires come back and swing the door
open. I hope everyone else is already outside...*

*But they're not. I fall on the ground, still cough-
ing and sweating, and I don't see nobody. I get up
from the ground and look back at my home, the
only one I've had for four years, burning to the
ground. Nothing but a big flame.*

"What did you do?!"

*Ms. Beefield grabs me out of nowhere. I jump
and when she swings me around to face her I see
that's she's really, really mad.*

*"How could you do this? Why did you do this?
This is YOUR fault!"*

She's yelling at me and I'm yelling back.

"I don't know! I'm sorry! I'm sorry!"

*She's screaming and I'm screaming. And then
her hands on my arms catch fire. She's screaming
some more and so am I. Then all of her is on fire.
Screaming. Fire. Screaming and Fire. I'm crying
and she's burning. She's burning because I'm crying.*

Because I did do it.

I wake up then. Not a big "Oh Mystics!" type of
wake up where you are screaming and in a cold
sweat, but just my eyes open and I'm lying there
like "This again?" You'd think I'd be over that nightmare because of what's happening now, but it never
fails to show up every once in a while and remind
me about what happened. Why can't I have normal
nightmares? Stuff like ghosts or evil killer androids

like normal people? No, I've got to have nightmares about my powers going nuts and making the worst night of my life even worse.

I get out of the bed and walk to my bathroom. I still have to get used to having my own bathroom, but on nights like this it's good to not have to walk through the house waking up Ms. Lynn or Mr. Isaac. I cut on the light and after my eyes adjust I look at my face in the mirror. The scared little brown skinned redhead from my dream is gone; instead a little older, but way less scary brown skinned redhead is in the mirror. One thing hasn't changed though. I snap my fingers and look at the flame that appears at the tips. These powers. They were "a blessing from the Mystics" according to Ms. Beefield. "How can I be mad to have one of the legendary Elementals under my care?" she had said after the fire. I wonder if I had actually burned up the whole shelter and her would she have still felt that same way. She never did explain exactly what "one of the legendary Elementals" actually was. For all I know they are a bunch of freaks with crazy destructive powers. They have to be; how could they be anything good if I'm one and my biggest achievement was burning up a kid's shelter?

I was having a nightmare that night too. Only this one scared me so bad that my body shot out fire instead of just dreaming about it. Sure, Ms. Bee didn't blame me, and Paul and Tevin actually thought it was cool when they were allowed to come back to the room, but I knew I couldn't stay. Not as long as a bad dream could turn me into a fireplace. I sigh and wave my hand so the fire disappears. No use worrying about it now; I have this power and there's no getting rid of it, so I might as well get over it. I turn off the bathroom light and try to go back to sleep.

Maybe the Lees had the right idea, getting rid of me.

#

The next morning, I wake up to Ms. Lynn cooking some breakfast. I follow the smells to the kitchen and watch her for a second. I almost feel bad for her. Since the schools here closed she has nothing to do in the mornings so she just cooks. She hates cooking almost as much as she hates not having a school to run, but once the androids wrecked the school she didn't really have a choice but to give up her job. Ms. Lynn turns around and sees me standing in the doorway. She fixes her head wrap and smiles at me.

"Good morning, Ms. Lynn," I say to her.

"Good morning Derren. How did you sleep?" She knows I have nightmares, but I lie anyway.

"Fine. When you've slept on the ground, any night in a bed is a good night." I sit down at the table to watch her.

She frowns a little as she scrambles some eggs. She hates the fact that I spent so much time on my own almost as much as she hates the Lees for ditching me in the first place. "I only wish we had met you sooner. You shouldn't have had to live like that at your age."

I start to tell her that I was living on my own at eight, so doing it again at twelve was nothing, but I let it go. "Where's Mr. Isaac?" I ask instead.

"He's getting ready for work," she answers. "Oh no..." the lights had just flickered and her old stove, the one that she said she and Mr. Isaac had ever since they got married, had turned off. "Another power surge...Derren honey, could you...?" I get up because I know what she's about to ask. My heart is already beating fast. "All I have left is finishing these eggs," she puts on an oven mitt and holds the skillet out far away from her, waiting on me to finish heating it up.

I take a deep breath and put my hand under it. They both love to get me to do little stuff like this, but it never turns out right. I shouldn't be using these powers at all; they're too dangerous, but they insist. I close my eyes and focus on making as small a fire as I can. Nothing too big, just enough to finish the eggs. I hear the flame crackling and her scraping the skillet so I know it must be working. I opened up my eyes and see Ms. Lynn whipping the eggs over the pretty small fire in my hand. I breathe out and even start to smile. Maybe I am finally getting the hang of this...I don't even notice the fire getting bigger until it starts to take over the skillet. Apparently, neither does Ms. Lynn.

"Oh!" Ms. Lynn gasps, snatching the skillet away and spilling some eggs on the floor. I close my hand as quickly as I can and the fire disappears.

"I'm sorry! I'm so sorry!" I say to her.

"It's fine honey, just fine. Thank you. I finished the eggs," she said with a slight smile. I looked in the skillet and saw that a few of the eggs are burnt. I feel myself getting mad. Why do they always do this? They should know by now that my powers never work right. Why keep making me use them? She must can tell I'm upset, because she pats my face with her hand and puts the eggs on the table.

I look up to see Mr. Isaac walking downstairs in a navy-blue shirt and some khakis. Since he works a few towns over his job is still safe, but he still watches the news every morning before he goes to

work to make sure that the androids haven't out-
lawed the bus system. Like every other morning he
speaks to us, goes to the living room, and turns on
the TV loud enough for us to hear it. He always sits
down so close to the screen I could practically watch
the news lady off the reflection on his bald head, so
that's what I do.

"...if you're just joining us, we are reporting that
Harold Carson, president of the Great Lands, has
been killed. On his way to meet with several world
leaders about the A.G. problem, he was murdered
by the android goddess herself. President Carson
will be succeeded by..."

The TV keeps talking but I don't think any of us
are listening anymore. Mr. Isaac looks at us and we
look back at him, so I decide to be the one to ask.
"What does it mean? If the president is dead then
what's gonna happen?"

"I don't know, Derren," Mr. Isaac admits. "Hon-
estly it's not like it really mattered that he was alive
before. Once that thing got the Orange Scepter and
started building more of those machines she already had the continent under her thumb. It will
only—"

"Do you really think she has it? The Orange
Scepter?" Ms. Lynn interrupts. Now more than any
other time I wish I had stayed in school after I left
the shelter or at least listened more when Ms. Lynn
tried to teach me about Colorius history. But then
again who thinks that world history would be this
important?

"Yes, I do. There's no way she could be taking
over so easily if she didn't. That android thing has
got to be stopped Lynn; it's going to be the death of
us all," Mr. Isaac sighs. "I think I'm gonna skip
breakfast this morning and head on to work."

Ms. Lynn wasn't having that. "You're going to die if you don't eat something before you go to work!" Ms. Lynn yells at him. Mr. Isaac knows better than to argue, so he just sits at the table with me and starts grabbing food. I decide to bring back up the thing I know we're all thinking about anyway.

"If A.G. is so powerful, who's gonna stop her?" I remember the way she had taken over some of the other continents like it was nothing. "Somebody's gotta do be able to do something, right?" Ms. Lynn stops in the middle of scooping some rice on Mr. Isaac's plate and he stops before he can put a strip of bacon in his mouth. They look at each other and Ms. Lynn nods. She sits at the table on the other side of me and Mr. Isaac puts his food back on the plate.

"What do you know about the Elementals, Derren?" Ms. Lynn asks.

I wasn't expecting this. "Nothing. I just know that Ms. Beefield, the lady at the shelter where I was, said that she thought I was one." Truthfully, she had said how the Elementals were heroes and great people and all but I figured she was just trying to make me feel better.

Ms. Lynn nodded. "Whenever bad stuff happens in Colorius, it's usually a group of people that protect all of us. When the Great Global War happened, when the Pewter Guard was assassinating people, all of that was stopped by the Elementals."

"So, what does this have to do with anything?" I ask, but I feel like I already know the answer.

"You asked who was going to stop A.G., and well son, *you*," Mr. Isaac says.

"What? Me? How? How am I supposed to stop that thing?!"

"The same way you cooked the eggs earlier. Your powers are different from other people's, stronger. You have Elemental powers, and those make you one of the people chosen by the Mystics to protect the world," Ms. Lynn explains. I do remember there being a kid who practiced magic at the shelter, but he couldn't do much more than change the channels on the TV with his power. I had torched a whole room on accident. But still...

"You're kidding, right? This is some joke? You guys can't really expect me to do something about A.G. by myself —"

"You wouldn't be by yourself. There's usually about ten Elementals. All of them about your age, all of them working together to do whatever the Mystics need them to," Mr. Isaac said.

"Why are you just now telling me this? Why didn't you send me to army school or something if you expect me to be some hero? Why not be teaching me how to really do some damage instead of having me cook eggs and light fireplaces?" It comes out harsh and I know it, but I don't really care. Who just springs this on people?

Mrs. Lynn leans over the table and grabs my hands. I look in her eyes and see just how serious she is. "Do you know why we didn't? Why we didn't give you to someone else who could help you learn our powers better, even after the specialists suggested it?" I shake my head. "You asked us were we going to give you up too. Soon as we left the doctor you asked Isaac and I were we gonna abandon you. I told you no and I meant that. Elemental or not, nothing was going to convince me to put you through going to another home. Isaac and I decided right then that we would keep you and teach you as much as we could."

"When this A.G. thing got serious, we both knew it was only a matter of time before you would start asking questions, before you would have to really be an Elemental. We decided that we would tell you when you asked, and now that you have its time for you to know." Mr. Isaac puts his hand on my shoulder and both of them smile at me.

I sit back and think for a minute. This is a lot. Last night I was mad that I had these powers, and now I'm supposed to use them to save the world. Who would've thought? I bet the Lees didn't know when they decided they didn't want me. Or maybe they did and decided I wasn't worth the trouble. Probably didn't think I could do it, or that I would even wanna do it. But here I am.

"Where would I even start? Would I have to meet the other Elementals? How would I find them?" I don't even know if Ms. Lynn and Mr. Isaac can answer these questions.

"All of that will happen when it's supposed to happen," Mr. Isaac says. "I remember watching a special on the last Elementals and some of them said that they met in a mall randomly. Remember, this is all the Mystics' plan, so when they're ready for you to meet them, you'll meet them."

"But it's not gonna be today, so eat that breakfast!" Ms. Lynn says, scooping me some more eggs and bacon on my plate. "You have got to be strong for whenever the time comes!" She smiles at me again and I smile back. It's great having someone who actually trusts me. The Lees might not have thought I was worth it, but Ms. Lynn and Mr. Isaac are different. It's sad they see more in me than the people who had me did.

"I've gotta go Lynn, I'm gonna be late for work!" Mr. Isaac gulps down his orange juice and stuffed some eggs and bacon between two pieces of toast.

"Okay, be careful honey! You saw the news," Ms. Lynn says. She kisses him and he heads for the door.

Mr. Isaac notices that I'm still pretty quiet so he looks at me and says, "Don't worry about it too much son. You may be hearing the hero call now, but everything is going to happen in time." He opens the door to walk to his car but freezes in the doorway.

"Civilian! You are hereby ordered into service under Queen A.G.!" a voice yells from outside. Mr. Isaac slams the door shut and looks at Ms. Lynn's and my terrified faces. He says the words he doesn't even have to say.

"There are androids outside."

#

Almost as soon as he says it the house starts to shake. The androids must be firing their laser blasts at the house, but thanks to the reinforcements Mr. Isaac and his friends put on it when they took me in, it would take a minute before they could get in.

"Go through the back door!" Mr. Isaac screams. Ms. Lynn grabs me and yanks me out of my chair so quick I barely have time to realize I'm moving.

"Come on Derren! We have to leave!" she says as she pulls me through the house.

"Ms. Lynn what if this is it?" I ask. I snatch out of her grip right before she can open the back door. "You guys said it was my job to help fight A.G., what if it starts right now?"

"We can't test that right now, Derren, if they kill you then what? We have to go!" she yells back.

"Civilians! Step out of the home and we will escort you peacefully into Queen A.G.'s service!" The androids seem to have realized that just blasting the house wasn't working so well, so they're trying to reason with us now. Mr. Isaac hobbles up to the back door and asks why we aren't halfway to Center City by now. Ms. Lynn explains that I have a death wish.

"I'm not running from them! If I'm gonna be an Elemental hero then I have to stand up to them!" I say to him. I'm still nervous and I don't even know if I believe what I'm saying, but I just feel like I can do this. I can show Ms. Lynn and Mr. Isaac that I can be the hero they think I am.

Since the windows aren't nearly as strong as the walls, the androids come to the side of the house they start firing laser blasts through the big one in the living room. Ms. Lynn screams and Mr. Isaac forces both of us to the ground. Under his arms I see two androids climbing through the shattered window. "Civilians, this is your final warning. Come peacefully to Queen A.G. or we shall exercise force." They lift up their hands, showing the clear circles in their palms that fired laser blasts.

I push Mr. Isaac off of me and against all better judgement and against Mr. Isaac and Ms. Lynn's screams, I throw fire at the one closest to me. Nervous or not, I am sure of one thing. They are not gonna get us without a fight. Both of them stumble backwards as the one I hit struggles to put out the flame.

"Unknown civilian has above average abilities. Take him alive," the burning android says to the other one.

I'm still so shocked that it worked I can hardly think. "You guys get outta here! I can handle them!" I say to Mr. Isaac and Ms. Lynn. Ms. Lynn reaches out for me but Mr. Isaac pulls her away so they both can get out. With a big smile on my face I turn back to the androids to see both of them shooting their lasers at me. The two blasts hit me and I fall down hard. From the ground I throw some more fire, but it barely hits the androids. My smile is gone now; I may be in trouble.

"Civilian's abilities are poor. He is not worthy to serve under Queen A.G. Exterminate him." I get up from the ground just to see some more androids coming in through the window. I try to throw some more fire at them but I get hit with two stronger blasts. Those two tore big holes in my shirt, and I get mad enough to throw some more fire, which completely misses. I realize the house is now on fire from all the flames that missed, giving me flash-backs of last night's dream. I realize I lost before I even get hit with the three laser blasts that knock me out.

#

"Hey you! Come back!"

I run out of the restaurant scarfing down as much of the table bread as I could. It was their own fault. Don't they know that the world is coming to an end? They should be trying to give out food to people. I finally stop running when I turn a few cor-ners and end up back in Rumas, far from my favor-ite restaurant. Almost on cue, the emotions start.

It's been about a month, but the memories of that day replay in my head even more than the night at the shelter. Waking up in a wrecked house.

Running out of it and down the street. Seeing Mr. Isaac's car a little ways down the road, still on fire. Praying to the Mystics that they weren't inside and it not being heard. Crying, not even knowing what to do with the bodies. Not knowing what to do with myself. The makeshift funeral, and back on my own again. Not having Ms. Lynn and Mr. Isaac anymore hurt more than anything I can remember, but I was determined to keep going. Even if it meant doing what I used to do back in the day: stealing, hustling, and hiding to survive.

I wipe a few tears out of my eyes and keep walking down the street. Things are so different now. People are still trying to live their lives, but more and more their lives are being wrecked by A.G. and her androids. I remember before how there were only the normal conspiracy theorists standing on the corners shouting at folks, now there are people begging for food and shelter to go along with the ones begging for attention. I realize that it's getting late and the news would be coming on soon, so I start to head to downtown Rumas. I always try to keep up with it so that I could know what that thing is doing next, and since I don't have a house anymore I have to watch it with all the other homeless people. I turn a few more corners and take up my usual spot on the street. I look up at the news station building and wait for the screen on top of it to start playing the news. Sure enough, it starts right on time.

"Hello and welcome to Nightly News with Kelvin James. Tonight, we continue our coverage of the "Terror of A.G.". Two of our sister stations, one in Oreton and another in Greater Grandia, are reporting even more missing persons. We urge viewers to please keep safe by complying with the androids' requests, and if at all possible, remove yourself from any place where they are known to congregate. We go to Rebecca Smite with some of the most recent android hotspots..."

"That thing is gonna be the death of all of us." Some old guy starts fussing as he walks by me and I completely get pulled out of the screen. "I can't wait until the Elementals finally get their acts together and take this thing down."

"Who says the Elementals can take her down?" I ask him. The man stops walking and looks at me like I have three heads or something.

"What did you say boy?"

"I said who says the Elementals can take her down. You see what she's doing out here! She killed like three presidents already and ain't stopping any time soon! I'm just saying, might as well not get your hopes up!"

The man shakes his head at me before he answers. I think he thinks I'm a little off in the head. "You must don't understand how Colorius works. The Elementals help us. Period. They're planning something right now; I promise you that. They're gonna show up and make that thing sorry, just you watch. They always come through. No matter what. Always, just you watch..." he starts walking away from me repeating "just you watch" like he's trying to convince himself.

I look up at the screen and realize that now they're talking about the weather, so I missed the major stuff. Stupid dude. I ball up the trash from my food and throw it in the closest compacter, and as the trash flies out of my hands it catches fire. I rush to try to stop the flaming ball of trash from getting any bigger, but it dies out before I get to it. Figures. My powers can't even burn trash well. No wonder I lost to those androids. That of course took me back to that day, and I realize again how wrong that guy was. The Elementals won't help him or anybody else because the Elementals suck right now. I keep walking by a woman with a big sign in one hand and a bunch of fliers in the other, screaming at the top of her lungs.

"The inventor of A.G. is still hiding in the city! Join the movement! Find him and bring him to justice!" the woman with the fliers is screaming at me and all the other people walking by her on the street trying to catch somebody's attention, and she just caught mine.

"What did you say?"

She smiles. I'm probably the first person to actually listen to her all day. "The man who created A.G. and sent her after all of us is still living in the city! We are trying to gather up more people to protest outside of his house and encourage somebody to do something about him! Do you want to join our cause?"

I grab one of the fliers she hands me. Suddenly I have an idea.

#

Okay. Just like you practiced. It will be fine. Just get in there and do like you practiced. Do it for them.

I raise up a shaking hand and knock on the door. It only took a couple days for me to work up the courage to actually come to this guy's house, but I probably should've taken longer to figure out what I would do when I got here. Was I going to burn the house down? Cry? Bring an army? I don't know, but

I know I had to see the guy responsible for A.G. and all these deaths for myself.

It takes so long for someone to come to the door that I knock again. This time a kid opens the door. He's shorter than me and has some blonde bangs that cover his eyes. "Who are you?" he asks.

"My name is Joshua. I am trying to raise money for homeless kids. Do you have any Redd Tokens you can spare?" I shake a small bucket with a few coins inside of it to sell the lie.

The kid looks at me and shakes his head. "No, sorry." He tries to close the door but I put my foot in it.

"Are you sure? Is there anyone else at home I can ask?"

"No. I'm here alone. My dad is out, sorry." He tries even harder to close the door on me, but I'm way stronger than this scrawny guy. Still, he said something I needed to hear.

"Your dad is out you say? Umm...well I can come back later. When do you think he'll be back?"

The kid stops trying to close the door and looks at me. "Why do you wanna know when my dad is coming back? Who are you?" This kid may be smarter than he looks.

I stop for a second and wonder what I should say. I decide to tell part of the truth. "Okay...here it is. I'm not raising money. My parents were killed by some androids, and I just-I need somewhere to stay for a little while. You are the first person to open the door, and..." I trail off and look down to make my-self sound really sad.

It works. The kid opens the door up wider and he looks even sadder than I hope I do. "Come in," he says. "My name's Morgan. You can relax for a little while. I know it has to be hard out there." He steps to the side to let me into his kitchen.

"Thank you so much Mor..." I stop talking because I can't believe what I'm seeing. Walking around in the living room is an android. I mean, yeah, she looks like a woman, but that's an android. No woman I have ever seen walks like that and has features like that. Looks that...wrong. My eyes follow when it sits on the couch, not paying attention to me at all.

"What's wrong?" the kid asks me. Does he not see the thing on the couch?! "Oh, sorry. I...I know you must be uncomfortable around androids, but Lauryn's good!" When I don't say anything he just keeps talking. "I'll turn her off now."

I'm just standing here in shock when he walks over to her. What do I do now? I didn't expect him to have a bodyguard. Why does he have one of these things in the house? Why did he name it? Are there more here? I'm so lost in thought I barely hear him say something to me.

"Joshua? Did you hear me? I turned her-what are you doing?!" the kid screaming at me shakes me out of my thoughts, and it isn't until then that I realize that my hands are balled up into fists by my side. Flaming fists. "What are you?!" he yells out, backing away from me.

This is it. Really, really it. This is the moment. The one Ms. Lynn and Mr. Isaac were talking about. The moment where I have to act. Even if it isn't doing anything, just having an android around these other people is dangerous. It has to be stopped. Him too, if I have to.

I pick up my fist to flick a flame at Morgan. Not a big one, just enough to try to scare him. If he's smart he'll leave here and let me destroy this thing and find his dad. The fire leaves my finger tips and rushes at Morgan. My aim is terrible, so instead of getting on his clothes like I wanted it heads towards his face. I have about a second to feel bad when the kid puts his hands up in front of his face.

Then the fire stops.

This faint whitish blue light shines in his hands and I feel a burst of cold air that hits my flame, putting it out. We both freeze for a few seconds trying to figure out what happened. Then I have the wildest idea, one I can't believe is actually about to come out of my mouth until it does.

"Are you an Elemental?" I ask him.

He is really scared now. He's shaking his head and takes off down the hallway away from me. I take a second to try to register this. If he *is* an Elemental he's supposed to be a good guy, right? But he has an android in the house, so he can't be that good, right? Unless...are there bad Elementals? Is he working for A.G.?

I realize that I'll never know if all I do is stand here, so I decide to flush him out. If he's an Elemental he'll be able to save himself again, right? If he's good then the Mystics will show him that this is his moment just like They're showing me that it's mine. If he's not good, well, I'll be one step closer to doing what an Elemental is supposed to do. I throw my fist towards where they walked to the back of the house and watch as the flames race down the hallway after Morgan. Finally, these fires do something useful.

FALLEN ANGELS

BY

ALAN JONES

Year: 2243

I am the Alchemist. This is why they call me. This is who I am.

I was in the midst of a waking dream, navigating the dream of another, when the siren brought me back to the present consciousness. I heard my cousin Darnell over the loudspeakers, "We have a level one incursion. I repeat, we have a level one incursion. All Jump team members please report to the launch room immediately!"

I was dressed and out of my room in less than a minute.

Our worldwide observation system, which some might call latter day cloud sitting, had detected an incursion. A powerful being from our off-world watch list had just arrived on earth. While others like us typically battled demons who sought life in the realm of flesh and blood, my family, known as "House of Sacrifice", also had responsibility providing protection from hostile aliens; many of whom had in past propped themselves up as gods to the ancients. I arrived in the launch room first and asked Darnell, "What's up?"

"Take a look." Darnell replied, as he began gathering items for the flight. "Akina just teleported there to do some recon. I'm going out to the ship to prep it. Bring the others when they arrive."

Just as Darnell exited, my daughter Rachel entered the room.

"Who?" Rachel asked quickly as she continued to fasten her garb.

"Nemesis and an unidentified companion." I replied.

"So, the chickens have come home to roost, eh?" Rachel sighed.

"Yes, they have." I answered.

Present that day were, Rachel (ageless warrior with a special suit of armor), my cousins Darnell (all around hero), Reggie (indestructible strong man), Akina (the Time Walker), Kim (electromagnetic powers), Nick my oldest (could transmute the state of any molecule) and Elizabeth (fire starter), Nick's childhood friend from the academy.

Nemesis was the Greek goddess of vengeance. She existed not to protect the Olympians, but rather to avenge them, should they ever fall. It was her sole reason for being. Her presence was concerning, but not totally unexpected since the Aunties were off planet. My mother Sarah and her sisters Cil, Deborah and Ruth had destroyed her home world Olympus, and killed the remaining old gods there, nearly a hundred years ago. However, many of the children and other descendants from these gods were not present and escaped that Armageddon. Thus, whenever the Elders sent the sisters across the universe to eliminate some threat, they'd call some of us home to take up residence in Aunt

Ruth's place, Cloud Seven, to watch over the earth in their stead.

A negotiated peace between star faring civilizations had largely protected the earth from the time the old gods were forced from the out by our ancestors, until Poseidon returned in 1981 (he and his cohorts attempted to build an Omni Portal on earth, which would have resulted in our world being overrun with ravenous creatures from every dimensions). Breaking this truce cost the sea god his life. As a matter of protocol for the death of a god, Olympus launched a full-scale attack against the earth. The Aunties repelled them and then at the direction of the Elders retaliated by traveling to Olympus and leaving only once it was dust beneath their feet. The Olympians were not the last civilization to suffer such a penalty, as the Elders decided that a message needed to be sent that would last across the ages. One after another the enemies of earth toppled across the heavens.

The remainder of the team arrived at the control room one by one. Reggie, who was lodging separately down at the lagoon, rode his motorcycle into the control room. When he entered, Nick and Rachel were hovering over my shoulder as I scrolled through data on my monitor. Reggie commented, "Ah, I see that the Wonder Twins are indeed here."

This is what Reggie called them, even though they had no reference for the moniker. Still, it seemed to amuse Reggie every time he said it, so he did. Upon his arrival to Cloud Seven a week before, he'd not ventured from his station at the beach. If you wanted to see him, you had to go to him. I did. My kids did not. Long story.

Nick and Rachel mumbled almost in unison, "Hi, Cousin Reggie."

As Reggie was dismounting his bike, in walked Kim and Elizabeth. One of the two seemed to have gussied up just a bit more than the rest of us. Reggie gave a quick glance towards the red headed Elizabeth, and then back towards Nick, before shaking his head in disbelief. It was obvious to all that they, over the years, had a thing for one another, but circumstances and commitments had prevented them from ever following through. Reggie liked to tease Nick about this fact. Rachel, who had simply affixed a baseball cap atop her head, and I, exchanged glances as well. But our glances were in regards to the fact that the world could be ending, but this child took a minute to fix herself up a bit before joining us. Elizabeth was in a relationship at the time, but as Chris Rock used to say back in the day, "You never know."

While boarding our low orbit transport it was decided that Darnell would pilot and play center field for this mission. Besides the fact that most of Darnell's powers wouldn't kick in until after sunset, it was our way to leave at least one resource just off the battlefield to watch everyone's back. If things happened to go south, Darnell would join the conflict using weaponry built into our craft, or if the battle raged into the night, he could swoop in himself. It was odd for us to engage pretty much every alpha and beta level resource in the compound for a mission; however, Nemesis was a level one threat, and she had backup with her. We hoped that they were acting alone and that this wasn't part of some larger invasion. Once in the air, it would only take us twenty minutes to arrive. Akina, who can easily walk across time and space, went ahead of us to assess the situation. Once in the air, Darnell called back to the others from the cockpit, "Akina has eyes on the second threat, you'll see her visual in a second."

Elizabeth gasped, "That's Magni, isn't it?"

Nick confirmed, "Yes, that's him and he has his father's hammer."

At his father's death, the Norse godling had inherited Mjolnir as his birthright. With it, he was just as big a threat as Nemesis. Our hands would be full with these two scions from realms long since dispatched by our aunts, at the direction of the Elders.

Kim shouted back over the din of our thrusters, "I hope Akina can keep them entertained until we arrive."

I noted that both aliens were from star systems starved for the element iron, and thus, Oxygen was no more to them, than Nitrogen is to us humans. So, I started figuring, "Hmm..."

My daughter Rachel tilted her head and asked, "What?"

"Just thinking on something." I said softly, lost in thought.

Once we'd completed discussing our plan, Reggie leaned in towards me and asked, "Hey, Black Jesus," that was what Reggie sometimes called me. He had nicknames for pretty much everyone. "You still doing that manna from heaven thing?"

His reference was to the fact that in my outreach work on other worlds, I did indeed convert commonly found matter into foodstuff that the locals could eat.

"Black Santa, you know that I still do." Black Santa was Reggie's nickname within the team. I asked, "Sure, you don't want to try some?"

"Naw, cuz I'm good. I wonder how anyone eats that stuff." Reggie answered.

"You get hungry enough, and there will be little to wonder about." I replied.

Reggie nodded and then shifted gears asking, "Y'all heard who the new Elder in waiting is, right?"

Kim lifted her head from her tablet, "Another *Immortal*, right?" Immortal within our community referenced those of us who did not age. No one on our team used that term about ourselves, but that term was how many of these individuals referenced themselves.

"Yep," Reggie replied.

Elizabeth shook her head, "So, that will mean that eleven out of twelve Elders will be ageless. I'm so not cool with that."

It wasn't a rule, but historically, of the twelve elders, it was seldom that more than four of them were ageless.

Nick chimed in, "The reasoning is that having less turnover will result in more consistent policies and practices."

Rachel reflected and nodded, "Well, yeah, I hear that, but..."

I jumped in, "Yes, the point is well taken, but while it may sometimes be uncomfortable, stirring the pot every now and then is healthy."

Reggie put a bow around the conversation, "It smells, don't it cuz?"

As we descended, Nick, as he often did, even when the Aunties were in play, took the lead. Both he and his sister Rachel served as officers in the earth's star fleet, he as captain, and she as a chief medical officer. She'd left the Corp some time ago to start a family, but Nick lived and breathed it just as much as ever. Everyone listened to his instructions, with the exception of the big burly Reggie, who had engaged in far more of these battles than anyone present.

Once Nick finished laying out our final instructions, Reggie crowed, "So, basically, get them, but don't get got."

As we broke through the rain clouds we saw the two giants in the midst of causing mayhem on an epic scale. Golden skinned, with black twists dangling, Nemesis was busy trying to stabilize a shiny metal contraption as energy arched from the clouds into it. Akina buzzed around her like a gnat, jumping in and out of this level of existence. The device Nemesis held was just as tall as she was, and just as wicked looking.

Elizabeth stood up, "That's a planetary drill! They're trying to destabilize the earth's core. Open up the back, I'm jumping out!"

Darnell did as Elizabeth requested and she flew down to join Akina. Over our communicators, we heard Akina tell her, "I was able to make the feet for that damn thing go bye-bye, but I can't grab a hold of the device itself to teleport it somewhere safe; too much energy."

Nick replied back to Akina, "Stand down Akina. You're too valuable to all concerned."

Nick said this in reference to Akina being the only resource on our team that could instantaneously ferry personnel across the universe. Thus, at the direction of the Elders, she was not to engage in direct combat. But let's just say that following orders, was never really something that Akina exceled at.

The red headed Elizabeth, flew low over Akina giving her a quick smile, before arching back up towards Nemesis, "I think girlfriend here could use a facial, don't you?"

Elizabeth proceeded to unleash a torrent of flames into the face of Nemesis. While the flames startled Nemesis at first, they weren't hot enough to harm her, much less ignite her flesh. But they were distracting enough to cause her to take a moment to adjust. Matter from her head ban descended down her face to form goggles around her eyes. By artificially expanding the electromagnetic range which she could perceive, they literally allowed her to see through the flames, to her tool of destruction.

Nemesis spoke aloud in the universal tongue, "Here to save the day, are you, righteous as you are? I will concede that we are a warlike people with little regard for human life, but so are you. You are no better than us. And now that you carry your destructive ways into the stars, you are no worthier of life than us. Welcome to Armageddon earthlings, we've had our fill!"

As this was happening, Darnell struggled to deposit us near the Magni, but the Norse god, was busy alternating from stoking the raging storm he'd brewed up and striking the ground with Mjolnir. Nemesis had a plan, but Magni simply wanted to smash as much stuff as possible.

Reggie instructed Darnell, "Just pull up and hover above his head and I'll jump out."

Darnell did as he asked and Reggie, along with his trusty club, leapt out of the cargo bay and onto the head of Magni. As Reggie landed he swung his club down into the Norse god's metal helmet. The impact was such that a low bass clang could be heard across the battlefield, even over the raging storm. The space god swung to and from trying to dislodge Reggie. But the thing with Reggie was that even though he was a big man, who couldn't pass through a doorway without at least turning slightly, he was very agile; extremely so. If any of us cousins could dance on the head of a pin, it would be Reggie. Finally, Magni, grabbed the helmet from his head and tossed it, along with Reggie, into the tree line.

These events allowed Darnell to deposit the rest of us in between the two oversized combatants and return to the skies once again. But this is where things began to go off plan. As we entered the battlefield the software inside of Nemesis' head band began to assess those of us just joining the fight. In doing so, it alerted Nemesis, that I Michael, the one and only son of Black Sarah, was present.

Nemesis, paused for a moment in disbelief. In the universal tongue, she called out to Magni, "It is the alchemist, Michael, son of Black Sarah! What better way to avenge to our ancestors than to slay the only child of that devil woman before we destroy the world of her birth!"

Magni's reply of a wide grin needed no translation. He turned toward me and swung Mjolnir into mother earth causing her to split open. The breach shook all of us on the ground.

Akina, who had been standing atop a tall building which overlooked the battlefield, cried over her communicator, "Enough of this!"

"Stand down Akina! You know the deal." Nick barked at Akina. She wanted to grab a hold of these beasts and teleport them somewhere far away. The problem was that she had to be tangible to touch them, and like a bug she could be squashed either before she teleported them or after they reached their destination. And since we didn't really know how they breached our defenses to arrive on earth, such a tactic might not buy us anything more than a brief respite. But knowing Akina, we all knew that she was only going to stay on the sidelines for so long.

After witnessing the two giants marching in my direction, Kim looked over her shoulder towards me and joked, "Hey cuz, they seem excited to see you. Do you owe them money?" She then mounted her metal skateboard and soared into the air to confront Magni.

My kids, Nick and Rachel stood beside me. For me it was a mix of pride and horror. I was pleased on one level that their first instinct was to protect me, but that was absolutely last thing I would ever want in such a situation. I looked at them feigning puzzlement, before switching from teammate to Dad.

"Hey, y'all need to be over there taking care of that drill while they're focused on me. Now!"

As they ran off, Kim and Magni traded electrical charges, until both realized it was a futile exercise. Kim then focused her efforts on magnetizing Mjolnir in hopes of somehow making it more difficult for him to use it. All manner of metallic matter, such as steel pipes from underground and railcars from the rail yard, flew into the powerful hammer, but none of it seemed to impede Magni's progress.

Reggie re-entered the scene slamming his club into the heel of Magni, causing the giant to spin and swing Mjolnir down upon him. The force of the blow drove Reggie into the ground.

In the meantime, Elizabeth, reached into her bag of tricks repeatedly to stop Nemesis; realizing that the heat of her flame was nowhere near hot enough to stop him, but nothing seemed to work.

I called out to my teammates, "Guys, all of you, back off. Go take that drill out while we have the chance and leave these two to me. Just give me some room."

Sure, that was quite a statement to make given my circumstances, but it was not completely without merit. While I'd seen less combat than any of the others present, and my offensive skills did not compare to some, I played defense with the best of them. I was hard to kill, very hard to kill. Thus, I welcomed the attempt on my life.

Nemesis, was very powerful in her own right. She had the ability, within certain limits to adapt to any given situation. Marching towards me, she removed her goggles and unleashed a killing glance which caused every living thing around me to immediately wither. This was typically her finishing move; but our book on her stated that she sometimes did this as an opening move. As one who cannot age or deteriorate, it had no effect on me.

Magni took his shot next by calling a barrage of lightning strikes down upon me. The ground smoldered for acres all around me. Smoke rose to the heavens as Magni called on a wind to aid him in examining his handy work. At last in the clearing air they saw me. I smiled at them, and then in the universal language I shouted back angrily at them, "My turn!" I'm certainly not the destructive force that my mother is, but I can do a few things. I touched the ground liquefying it as far out as my two attackers, making the whole area essentially a huge tar pit. Then, just as soon as they splashed in, I changed it into a particular metallic compound to lock them in place. Magni, struggled mightily, even calling down a second round of lightning from the skies. But he could not free himself. Nemesis however was a different matter. At first, she too was trapped, but then I saw it. I saw her glow a blushing hue, just as our research stated she would do when she called upon her adaptive powers. She summoned the ability to change the state of molecules, the same as my son Nick. And in doing so, she changed the prison around her into its gaseous state and flew up into the air and landed next to her compatriot to free him as well. We were back where we started, or so it seemed. The two behemoths stood side by side facing me. I waited a moment, for the rest of my plan to play out.

The composite I'd frozen them in was relatively harmless to them in its liquid or solid state. But in its gaseous state it binds with Oxygen and subsequently forms a nearly unbreakable material that solidifies when it came into contact with their alien flesh. With a quickness, their own skin became a metallic prison, and even if they managed to transform this new compound into gas or liquid, it would literally rip away their flesh. And by their still being on the relatively cool earth the substances would simply solidify upon them again. While their artificial respirators continued to supply the molecules they needed to remain alive, they were little more than statues. Their glistening faces were turned towards the setting sun as the winds became gentle once again. It was quite a sight. I turned and began walking towards the prone planetary drill. From a distance, I could see that with a few quick blows the mud-covered Reggie had broken the planetary scalpel into several pieces. My son Nick worked to turn the chunks into a liquid which ran down the giant hole in the ground the drill had created.

Akina, Kim and Elizabeth joined me on the ground as I walked towards the others.

Elizabeth, who'd officially only joined our team that year, asked, "What now?"

Kim and I both looked off, before Akina answered, "Well, we used to hold intruders like these and negotiate some kind of terms with whomever they belonged to. But the current set of Elders really don't believe in diplomacy."

Kim asked, "Can't we just leave them like this and move them off world?"

I answered, "Well, their environmental packs should operate for years, but eventually, they'll run down and they'll suffocate."

I was quiet for a moment before I began again. "But now that they're powered down, with a touch, I could take care of this."

Akina touched my arm, "No cousin, let me handle this. I'll take them to the Pit. We can work out a safe way to unfreeze them later."

Given that I was a man of peace, and in fact a missionary serving in the less traveled corners of the universe, my cousins tried their best to protect me from the realities of our role as protectors of human-kind. In much the same way, in the previous generation, my Aunt Ruth was protected by her sisters because she was so tender hearted. By moving them to the "Pit", a place out of time, we were in layman terms, storing them in a place that was something of a purgatory. Releasing them there, they'd have to fight it out with the demons that existed there in the flesh. But these were powerful beings, and that at least provided them a fighting chance.

At last we reached Rachel, Nick and Reggie. Reggie staring up in the twilight at the frozen space gods, from atop the last chunk of the drill to be cracked, called out, "Good work Cuz. I'm impressed."

I replied with a smile. This is who I am. This is why they call me. I am the Alchemist.

SERKET

BY

VIOLETTE L. MEIER

Her eyes opened; shapes shifted and took form. Air was sucked into her lungs. Her chest expanded with sacred breath, and her spirit stirred within her. Space and time paused then resumed as she blinked. Tears rimmed her chestnut brown eyes that shined wide and full of knowing. Scarlet goo glistened from her pitch-black skin as she screamed to the top of her lungs.

"One more push!" the midwife instructed as she sat between legs trembling in pain. She cupped her hand to catch the life that was crowning before her eyes. Hair pushed from the womb, then a head, then a beautiful body perfect in every way.

"It's a girl," the midwife exclaimed as she held the tiny child above her head and thanked the great God for the new life in her hands. "Blessed be!" she shouted in exaltation and handed the baby to her mother. Kemet had birthed a new generation.

Queen Pebatjma, charcoal legs still spread wide and body soaked in sweat, kissed her daughter's gooey head and passed her back to Tuya, the midwife, to be cleaned. The queen fell back on her pillows and breathed easy for what felt like the first time in eons.

Queen Pebatjma had been in labor for sixteen hours. She timed it by Pharaoh Kashta's appearance every two hours. His intense anticipation seemed to make Pebatjma's contractions more forceful as if the child ached to see its father as much as he ached to see it. It had been an hour since he had last appeared with impatient eyes searching for a new development. Time rested deep into the night. The queen was almost positive that her husband was resting his head on his couch, by now, dreaming of holding his newborn son or daughter.

The old woman cleansed the baby in a basin of fresh water sprinkled with spices. She then wrapped the baby in swaddling clothes, heaped blessings upon her head, fastened a charm around the child's wrist, and took her back to her mother.

"What will she be called?" Tuya asked, a smile on her dark leathery face. Deep wrinkles creased the sides of her eyes and the corners of her thick lips. She was pretty for someone so ancient. Youthful eyes and a mouth full of sparkling white teeth solidified her beauty. Her body was short and stout with burly arms and strong legs. Her hair was braided like an intricate basket, full of textures, twists and turns forming a floral-like crown.

It was rumored that Tuya had delivered the pharaoh's babies for the past thousand years. Her name had been written in the histories for ages and there was not a royal alive who, nor their grandparents, did not know her. It is said that Tuya came from the southern lands, where all humanity had begun, into Kemet when the gods walked the earth. Legend claimed that she saw the sands give birth to the pyramids and that she knew Ra before he became a god. She was rumored to have seen the waters being separated from the waters and her feet was one of the first to step on dry land when it appeared. She was called Wisdom, wife of Knowledge.

It had been a long time since the gods had walked among the children of the earth. Only the pharaohs clung to divinity in a desperate attempt to control power, but Tuya remembered that there was a time when the gods truly walked the earth and her visions showed her that they would come back one day.

"I will call her Amenirdis," Queen Pebatjma answered while showering kisses upon her daughter's tiny head. "She is so beautiful."

"Indeed," agreed Tuya; nodding at the new mother and child with admiration in her eyes.

The baby was reddish brown like her father, Pharaoh Kashta, with a crown of wavy hair. Her face looked to be his as well, but it was much too early to tell; for babies morphed many times within the first year of their lives. It was almost a guarantee that she would grow up to be a striking beauty like her mother.

"Sweet child," the old lady cooed. "Indeed, blessed be."

The door swung open. Between the heavy muscled, topless guards, Tyti, a high-ranking house servant, walked into the room. She bowed to the queen and rolled her eyes at the old midwife.

"The child has come," Tyti stated with a look of chagrin. Her folded arms and disappointed eyes made Tuya cut her teeth.

"Shall I inform the king?" Tyti asked the queen, not removing her eyes from the wrinkly child in her arms.

"Let him sleep until I am fit for viewing," answered the queen. "I want him to see me at my best."

Blood and afterbirth soaked the linens beneath her and the marble floor surrounding her birthing bed. Soiled towels were scattered everywhere like dragonwort. Queen Pebatjma's bald head shined with perspiration; her braided wig sat on a nearby table spread out like a sleeping spider.

Tyti turned her nose up and let out a sigh of disgust as her eyes scrutinized the ebony queen and her clay colored baby.

Tuya's face twisted in anger as Tyti eyed the queen and her child. It was unfathomable why Tyti was not put out of the palace years ago. Spying was the girls second nature. Her devious green eyes seemed to be peaking around every corner, and miraculously moments after, the pharaoh would be told an altered version of what Tyti claimed to have witnessed. It was said that she was a worshipper of Set and she embodied a magic that was so diabolical that it would make even Anubis fear death. Tuya believed that maybe it was the girl's magic that held the pharaoh in her favor. That seemed like the only logical explanation that would keep the girl in the royal home. At first Tuya thought that the pharaoh fancied the girl, but there was no indication of an affair.

"May I clean up?" Tyti asked, her honey brown face wrecked with jealousy. It was no secret that she was in love with the pharaoh. She swooned at the sound of his voice and showered him with praises at every chance. Every night she envisioned herself in his arms instead of his wife. Tyti hated that her seductive advances were either thoroughly ignored by the king or that he was completely oblivious to any woman but his wife. Tyti found the pharaoh's fawning over his wife utterly pathetic. Every inch of Tyti was annoyed with the queens overly joyous and helpful disposition. It seemed like nothing ever got under the queen's skin. Yet, it was clear that Pebatjma only tolerated Tyti because her family had served the crown for generations. Tyti used her families' legacy to her advantage and manipulated every situation to her benefit.

Tuya had warned Pebatjma time and time again about the dangers of Tyti, but the queen would not get rid of the girl. Tradition and loyalty was everything to the queen; so, until Tyti was caught in wrongdoing, she would continue to serve.

"Yes, you may clean up," Queen Pebatjma answered, handing the baby to Tuya.

Tuya sat in the corner of the room with the baby pressed to her bosom in quiet observation.

Tyti pulled the basin filled with crimson colored water out of the room and returned with fresh water for the new mother to wash. A group of women came in to clean the chamber as Tyti helped the queen bathe. The smell of soap and perfume overtook the scent of birth and blood. Within an hour, the queen was dressed in a fresh tunic, gold cuffs glistened on her wrists, a hand carved choker embraced her neck, and bird shaped earrings dangled from her ears. She looked like an onyx goddess perfectly carved by the gods. The once blood splattered chamber now looked pristine, and the cleaning women left as quick as they had come.

Amenirdis began to cry.

"Time to nurse," Tuya said as she stood up.

Tyti rushed over to the old woman and said," Let me take the princess to the queen."

Tuya looked at Pebatjma and she nodded her permission for the baby to be handed to Tyti. Tyti roughly pulled the infant from the old woman's arms and sauntered over to the queen. The queen reached out her arms and the servant dropped the baby into them.

"Be careful!" the queen hissed. "Watch how you handle my child!"

"Clumsy me," Tyti mumbled, and rolled her eyes.

"It's time for you to leave," Tuya barked, her strong legs crossing the room in mammoth strides.

"You are not my authority," Tyti barked, her young face sneering and ready for attack.

The baby began to scream.

"Get out of here," the queen ordered; sweat bubbling on her forehead. "Guards!" the queen called.

Silence.

"Your guards are loyal to me! Never underestimate my womanly talents," Tyti guffawed with arms folded and head thrown back.

The queen and Tuya eyes met in panic. It was too much of a fragile time for battle.

"The pharaoh ordered me to bring him the child," Tyti lied; reaching out for the baby.

The queen slapped Tyti's hands away.

"Over my dead body!" the queen hissed, clenching the baby to her chest. "Your time here has come to an end. Out of respect for your ancestors, I have tolerated you. Leave this palace at once or I will gift you with your own head!" Admonition gleamed in the queen's eyes. If forced, she would gladly be a death dealer; for her delicate hands were full of strength and skillful danger.

"So be it! The pharaoh will be sickened by the loss of you and the child, but I will help him through his grief. I will offer him comfort like he has never known. What a spectacle the royal mourners will make over your cold dead body," Tyti seethed in anger as she pulled a vile from the top of her tunic, removed the lid, then tossed its contents at the queen. The dark, smelly liquid hit the queen's arm with a loud sizzle. She began to howl like her soul was being ripped from her flesh. A sprinkle of the poison hit the baby's lip and the child lapped it up like her mother's milk.

"No," Tuya screamed as she pushed Tyti to the floor a moment too late. Tuya rushed to the queen's side and frantically began to pray and chant seemingly worthless incantations over her wounds.

Pebatjma screamed, writhing in pain, her flesh bubbled like hot tar.

The child latched onto her mother's arm, like a breast, and sucked the poison out in frantic gulps. Tuya tried to pull the baby away, but the child was unmovable. Soon, Pebatjma's cries faded from a horrific wail to a faint whimper into a painless sniffle. She looked down at her daughter dazed and confused. Queen Pebatjma's arm was completely healed, and Amenirdis' countenance became more beautiful and vibrant than before. Her small features seemed to mature into a child half a year older.

Amenirdis turned towards the vicious servant and Tyti's smile was ripped from her face.

"Death!" the young woman squealed as she stepped backwards; her wide feet slapping the marble floor like drums.

The child pointed her newborn tiny finger at Tyti and a swarm of scorpions appeared out of the floor and surrounded her feet. The gold bangles on her wrists and arms morphed into serpents who sank their dripping fangs into the golden flesh of her arms and neck.

"Serket!" Tuya screamed as the scorpion's tails struck Tyti's feet over and over until they were two bubbling mounds of flesh. The young woman fell to the floor foaming at the mouth; her skin a putrid green and blistering in wet goo. Tyti's vacant eyes rolled backwards and she was gone.

"The goddess has returned!" Queen Pebatjma whispered as she held her baby at arm's length and looked into her omniscient eyes. The queen pulled the child back to her bosom and waited for her king to come.

Tuya fell prostrate before the child; singing hymns of praise with tears of joy.

Little Amenirdis smiled and turned to her befuddled mother's breast and latched on.

REAPING WILLOW

BY

AZZIZA SPHINX

"You can't change who he is."

Clyde's words slithered into my psyche reiterating the voice in the back of my mind reminding me that Death makes no apologies for who he is and what he does. I know my dear Nero has his reasons. Reasons of which I can never know or even remotely begin to understand. Nero's lie still stung, even if it was "selective omission" of minute details.

I huffed. My fingers tightened around the staff of my scythe. The tip of the sharp blade reflected the rays of sunlight peeking through the bearing branches of the willow tree a few feet away. Clyde was right. No denying it. I tried not to be naive. I wanted so much to think what Nero and I shared broke all of the rules. Yet, here I stood, facing down a demon of my own creation.

I was bound to Death, a choice of my own when I sacrificed myself to keep the balance of the universe after he broke *The Rules* by splitting his power among others. And after all these years, I thought I could trust him. Oh, how wrong I'd been. Our last argument hadn't ended well. I'd called his bluff, forcing his hand. And even though I'd have forgiven him if he'd told me the truth he maintained the ruse hiding behind words such as "selective omission."

"Lavenia?"

The concern in Clyde's voice drew me from my musings. His narrowed eyes roamed over my face, his expression serious. And Clyde was the serious one among us, Nero's squad of rogue Reaper collectors –the Wraiths of Reapers our adopted name. We acted as the clean-up crew when some unfortunate Reaper decided to deviate from *The List* and collect souls before their time. Billy was the playful one, the young spirit, next to the baby of our crew and only other female – Sira. And well, my place as Death's concubine and right hand was in question considering I'd turned my back and made it very clear I needed space; lots and lots of space.

With a mere thought, the blade of my scythe shimmered into pixie dust leaving the staff and its three mist filled orbs as my weapon of choice. Reaper or Wraith I needed to push the anger and frustration aside and focus on the task at hand. I hunkered down, feet spread, relaxed and prepared. I stared at my opponent, our eyes locking. Taunting. Teasing. A silent dare passing from him to me and back as anticipation grew thick between us. Who would make the first move?

My fingers twitched in eagerness to be the aggressor, and for once I gave in to the urge. In one fluid swoop, I swung my staff behind me, planting the end in the moist ground, heaving my body upwards onto the branch behind me. Taken by surprise at the retreat, Clyde's forward momentum placed him right beneath me. He'd expected me to come forward and so he planned to meet my stride. Had I done what he expected, our staffs would have collided at this exact position. Instead, he found me dropping down from above, my foot pushing him further forward as I pushed off his back in a turn, my staff making a cracking sound as it whacked into his back.

I noticed the smell of fresh rain on the ground as I rolled to regain my balance. Fingers outstretched, sliding across the forest floor I again stared at my adversary.

He bowed to me as he brushed the remnants of decomposing leaves from his pants. "Touché."

Not convinced this wasn't some trick to make me drop my guard, I stood at the ready for a moment more watching and patiently waiting for him to surrender completely. We'd been doing this for over an hour now, he coming out as the victor about as much as myself. I understood his need to keep me busy. *A troubled Reaper leads to fast-running sand.*

Eventually, he grew tired of the charade, and so he tossed his staff into the brush, hands raised in surrender. "Giving up so soon?" I said finally able to relax. My fingers rolled my staff before, with a brief consideration, I summoned the blade to return.

"Actually," he lowered his hands, shoving them in front pockets before leaning against the tree staring off into the distance intentionally avoiding eye contact. Strange.

"Clyde? What's going on here?" He'd moved on, so I banished my scythe. It burst into a spray of tiny little lights, glittering and twinkling as the energy burned away. It was a trick of the eye and my way of showing off. The others chose to play Houdini – now you see it, now you don't. I needed a little fanfare in my life. Not that bedding Death in the flesh wasn't full of excitement. But that was different. This was different. This was all mine. All me.

"You haven't been the same since..."

I cut him off because I knew where this was going and I was not going to have this conversation with him. It's none of his business. It's none of their business. "Since what?" The accusatory tone fit perfectly. He needed to understand me clearly. "Y'all act as if I've fallen apart since I figured out Nero's game."

"Death doesn't play games!" Clyde spat at me.

The words hit me hard. Not quite below the belt hard but hard enough to make me take a step back and give him the once over. He still avoided my gaze. His foot kicked a rock like a kid knowing he needed to tell his mother what happened but afraid of her wrath. And there it was. That mere thought smacked me in the back of the head. I realized that I was doing precisely what he implied.

Big girl here, I can admit my mistakes. I closed the distance between us my hand coming to rest on his arm so that he looked up at me. "Clyde, I am so sorry. You're right. I was angry, and I was taking it out on everyone instead of owning up to my role in this. I guess I did kind of believe that he would never lie to me. Or at least I hoped he wouldn't."

I could tell he understood my position. His pale fingers ran through his perspiration-soaked dark hair. Clyde tried his best to remain a neutral party, though many times that meant telling people what they didn't want to hear. He approached the subject tactfully, teetering on being diplomatic and yet fatherly. Age did that. Well, age and a stint in the mines in the Sands of Time.

"He is who he is Lavenia. Just as you are who you are." He pushed away from the tree, his demeanor serious. "But you two will not survive without each other. And neither will the world. That was part of the deal when you made your sacrifice. However," he patted me on the shoulder, "we can finish this conversation at a later time. We have a more pressing matter to tend to. One of which I need your assistance."

Clyde opened his palm to reveal a 2x2 sheet of parchment. Parchment meant mortal soul, human instead of the Reapers we typically sent back to the Sands of Time. When we received the call to reign in a Reaper, the message came in hourglass form. The name Rose was scribbled across the thin paper in old embellished Calligraphy. I hadn't seen one like it before, the script covered in extra lines and adornments. It reminded me of archived documents, items to be treasured not fondled like Clyde stroked this paper. No way could this be what he needed my help with.

"I can't believe you're asking for help with a human collection." The choice of words felt foreign on the tip of my tongue. Human collection was an odd choice, even for me. The words were old and stiff, something I might hear from my darling bedmate Nero. It made me wonder.

"You know as well as I do, things aren't always the way they seem."

"I agree." I crossed my arms eyeing him suspiciously. He ignored my scrutiny.

He turned from me and started to walk towards the stone staircase leading to the front door. I almost thought he wasn't going to respond until he said, "Get cleaned up and meet me in the garage in thirty."

I did as instructed, except I took forty-five minutes just to assert my authority. Yes, it was a risk. When Clyde set his mind to something, you either followed suit or stood by on the sidelines. But this time he needed me, which made this now my turf. And as a play on the saying goes: my turf, my rules. So, as I sauntered into the garage, I sashayed my way past him to the passenger side of the silver SUV with tinted windows careful to avoid looking in the side mirror. *Me and mirrors don't get along.*

Clyde slammed the driver's side door harder than necessary as he climbed in behind the wheel. By the time he secured his seatbelt, adjusted the seat and mirrors and started the vehicle, I was already tucked away behind the passenger's seat comfortably resting with my head back and eyes closed.

I waited until the road evened out before I ask my first questions. "Now." I paused, waiting to see if he cared to elaborate before I dove into my line of questioning. Silence. Guess not. "Are you going to tell me what this is about? I'd like to get a handle on what we are walking into if we really are walking into something."

He rambled on about the information I'd typically find inside the dossier collected with every soul from *The List* – the list of names of people whose time in this world had come to a close. Name, age, the supposed cause of death – though that one was flexible. We tried our best to follow the suggestions, but sometimes things just didn't go as planned. Today's target: Rose was 97. In her prime, she'd had a spell or two in a brothel but eventually married and bore six children, one of which she continued to live with, though the woman traveled a lot for business and made sure a nurse checked on her mother at least every other day.

Somewhere within the droning on of Clyde's voice the exhaustion I'd been ignoring for the last five days caught up with me. When I finally opened my eyes, the clock on the dashboard indicated my nap lasted precisely three hours and eighteen minutes.

"Why didn't you wake me?" I asked alarmed. He never said anything about us driving for hours before we left the house. Not that I bothered to inquire about where we were going. It really didn't matter so long as once we reached ourdestination, I got the chance to get a feel for the place and the plan.

"You needed the rest. You should have beat me more than you did. Billy told me about the insomnia. And Sira told me about the dreams."

Embarrassed – and a little ticked off - I stared out the window watching the landscape pass. I'd only told Sira the light parts of the dreams. About the memories of the time before the Sands of Time, when I reigned as the High Priestess of the Nai. It was my way of working through these new memories, memories stolen from me before my Prince, Rasul woke me from a horrible metaphysical block.

"Rasul is worried," Clyde said. "He says that since he brought you back, you've been avoiding him."

"Oh really? I've been avoiding him?" I'd thought we were in a residential area, but the closer I looked at the rows of houses, I realized that they'd been converted it businesses. A quaint little place with anunadorned sign reading Angelo's caught my attention when we stopped at a four-way stop. I cracked the window, the permeating scents of a unique blend of Italian and something else I couldn't quite place made my mouth water.

I turned back to Clyde. "We should come back to this place and eat."

He peeked over at the restaurant then made a right turn. "As you wish milady."

"Now tell me again why you need my help." I changed the subject because I didn't want to get into the details of the dreams and the avoidance. Though Rasul was the one avoiding me, I understood now that that was because of the angry black woman syndrome I'd thrust upon them the last few days.

"I don't have many details, all I know is that something about this one feels different. I tried consulting *The Book of Time and the Dead* but have run into a dead end. I figured, at the very least I needed to bring backup."

Backup huh? Interesting. "So why me? I mean, I would think that Billy would be at the top of your list. I remember the days when you two were inseparable."

"Well, those days are long gone. We aren't exactly seeing eye-to-eye on some things right now. Even Nero is starting to see it. Something is going on with Billy."

"All the more reason to keep him close." We were in a residential area now. The stretches between the houses growing. I started to see more offshoot street signs and neighborhood entrances the further out of the city limits we drove.

"Not in this case. I need someone who I know can watch my back."

"So why not Jesse? Or even Rasul? Why the broken priestess running on pure adrenaline?"

"You are not broken." He turned down one of the streets stopping short of the line of cars waiting to enter the complex.

"If you say so."

"Lavenia."

I knew he was looking at me in the mirror though I dare not shift my position to stare back at him. "Fine. Whatever. So, you think we have a fight on our hands?" My palm itched and not in that high anticipation kind of way. I knew this itch. It was a slow burn under the skin like something forming below but not quite ready to burst through the surface.

He eased forward, ignoring my query. Not that I expected him to respond. Just like Nero, sometimes quiet spoke the loudest. Silence was all the answer I needed.

The neighborhood consisted of eight houses. Each home sat on what I guessed was no less than four acres. I saw different combinations of swimming pools, tennis court, gardens and gazebos littering the yards, each I'm sure custom made to the specifications of their respective owners. We soon reached our destination, a real hoity-toity place at the back of a cul-de-sac with a massive stone house surrounded by another set of impressive iron gates.

To my surprise, Clyde pulled right up to the house, punched in another set of codes and proceeded to take the winding driveway around to the back.

"What are you doing?" I asked, uncomfortable with being seen. While our Wraith status meant we could mask ourselves from prying eyes, no way could we hide an SUV. It just wasn't possible.

"She's expecting us."

"Wait? What?"

He parked and slid out before circling the vehicle to let me exit. "Like I said, this one is different. She brokered a deal long ago, learning the exact date and time of her demise."

News to me. I followed him into the house. Our target was even nice enough leave the back door open. We crossed through the emasculate home adorned with floor to ceiling paintings of rose gardens and Fae. Eventually, we exited on the side which opened up to an extensive garden area with colorful sprays of roses in every hue. The beauty was unnatural. This woman either had a massive green thumb or a 24-hour a day gardener. Not a weed or darkened leaf in sight.

"You sure this woman is mortal?" Again, silence. "She isn't mortal, is she?"

Clyde stood beneath a trellis covered in gold and white roses, his arms relaxed to his sides as the wind tousled his hair. A few stray golden petals dances around him. It would have been angelic if he wasn't one of us. "You tell me."

I gave the place a visual once-over, trying to piece together the puzzle he presented. According to Clyde, our target, Rose, mostly lived alone. She had apparently done well for herself, or at the least maintained enough financial sense not to blow a considerable inheritance. This house couldn't have come cheap, and the care of the gardens themselves probably cost as much as the mortgage. Unless.

"She's a...?" My voice trailed off.

"A...?" Clyde refused to give me an answer.

"Rose." The word came out as confirmation rather than a question. The air around us stirred, the scent of the gardens smacking me in the face before growing heavy and forcing me to gasp for breath. Such power. Such full, unadulterated strength.

I'd been here before. Seven or maybe eight years ago. Long before I understood my role as the High Priestess of the Nai but long after being bound to this world as a Wraith. I stared Clyde down, hoping. Or maybe I was delaying the inevitable.

"Tell me what you remember," he said, apparently in no rush to claim our bounty.

I joined him beneath the arch of beauty, the wind died down as if the source desired to hear the story as well. A light breeze brushed against my cheek urging me to purge my soul of the words fighting to escape parted lips.

"Nero and I crossed *The Sands* seeking not a time stealer but a healer. Legends spoke of a keeper of Woz. At the time he was sure it would help me with the transitions. I don't think he was looking for a cure but something to buy more time while he determined the best path to finding me a permanent body in this realm."

"Is that what he told you?"

I shot him a quizzical glance. "You know Nero. He doesn't exactly 'tell' me anything, especially when it comes to my coming through the veils into this world. But he made me follow him. I could tell he wasn't happy to have me tag along, but I suspected that you all were busy, so he was stuck babysitting."

"Was this before or after you figured out who pulled you out of limbo."

Hmm. I had to think on this question. While I knew Nero limited access to my realm in-between realms -*The Void*- to only a few, I understood it took someone of Nero's power to open the link and pull me from it into the waking world. I'd never thought much of it. Just that when I did end up in my temporary vessel either Nero nor his counterparts waited for my waking.

"Before," I finally replied after piecing together the timeline.

"I can only say this much; I think when he brought you back that time he feared you might not return. We've all said that our rules do not apply to you. Some of that we chalked up to the female thing. The complexity of the psyche if you will."

"Why Clyde? Was that a 'smart' remark?"

"Ha. Ha. Funny. Not falling for that one. Anyway, it wasn't until I started to delve deeply into *The Book* did I piece together the link between the two of you. I mean, we've all heard bits and pieces of the story. Nero broke the rules. You sacrificed yourself. The powers that be decided to give Nero a taste of his own medicine in return. It all made sense on a high level."

"But?"

"However," It wasn't lost on me that Clyde chose a word other than 'but.' "there had to be more. I found clues in *The Book* about a formula, one that couldn't keep you in a temporary vessel for all eternity, but it held the potential to extend the length of time so that you wouldn't slip back into *the Void* so quickly."

Rustling to my right split my attention. A soft glow permeated from Clyde's palm. Not enough to draw the attention of the person daring an attempt to sneak up on us, but sufficient to let me know that he had my back if I needed him to. We continued our conversation, hoping that our visitor thought we were oblivious to his presence. "Do you believe his intentions honorable?"

"Interesting question."

The glow faded as the scent of roses grew stronger. I realized that the air around me stilled, though the undeniable aroma of the flowers draped over me. I allowed a bit of my power to spread, and like a moth drawn to an open flame a part of me escaped into the rose labyrinth behind us. It wove a path, stopping at two distinct points before doubling back to the center and then out again.

"They were," came a voice as soft as the whisper of winter wind through piles of fallen leave.

My enhanced hearing allowed me to discern the words. I don't know what I was expecting to see when I turned, but it undoubtedly wasn't the figure no more than four feet tall floating just above a wreath of fluttering blue rose petals standing before me. Her golden tresses waved in a self-contained breeze, her skin glowing like the beginning of sunrise. Cupped in her hands were three roses. One white. One black. One gray.

I stared at the delicate blooms, their colors melding then separating as if they shared one stem and water source where each flower drew a little or a lot of food coloring to fit its color. White roses grew everywhere. And I'd even seen a black one a time or two. But the gray one captured my attention. In between the black and the white, the edges of the gray that touched the white rose drew in white while the petals that brushed against the black appeared to repel that color.

My hand burned, my fingers curling over in a fist though I hid the discomfort from the woman hovering before me. "What does it mean?" I asked.

She smiled, her eyes darting to Clyde who stood over my shoulder watching the magic show. "You still do not understand?"

Understand? What was there for me to understand? We came here to collect a soul. Albeit willingly, I didn't see any difference in this case than any other.

The woman turned her attention back to Clyde, "She is awake is she not?'

"Yes."

"Then she should know."

"I should know what?"

Clyde placed a hand on my shoulder, his other hand extending to point at the three roses. "Tell us what you see?"

My hand hit my hip before I could stop it. "I see three roses. One white. One black. One gray."

"And what does it mean?" He asked.

"I don't know. It's three freaking roses." I let my frustration spill over into my voice. "What is it supposed to mean?"

Before Clyde spoke the next words, his scythe materialized. He shoved me so hard I took the woman down with me to the ground. Her hands folded between us, the roses crushing beneath the weight as a whoosh of warm air brushed across my back. I duck-crawled forward, dragging an unconscious Rose behind me by the arm. I tucked her as safe as possible behind a rose bush and summoned my scythe. The bright white burn drew the attention of the angry red-headedwoman barreling down on Clyde. He had his back to me, but I was sure he could see the pulsing of my scythe.

"Stay back Lavenia," he yelled as he blocked the blow of the swinging head of a mace.

I'd seen that weapon once before. I knew exactly who we were up against. This wasn't some random Reaper coming to dispose of a soul from T*he List.* This was personal. For a moment I thought Rose might have set us up, but I didn't have time to ponder the thought. The woman brought her leg down on Clyde's knee, sending him crashing down his arms wrapping around the now damaged appendage. His scythe faded away as pain consumed him breaking his concentration.

"So, we meet again?"

I readied myself for the fight at hand. "Willow." Her name fell from my lips with disdain. She was as strong as ever. Her figure was slimmer than the last time we crossed paths, and the more defined muscle structure indicated she'd trained for this moment. Our last meeting ended in a stalemate. Partially because of the interference of Nero. This time, however, I knew with certainty, she was going down.

"Fitting it ends here. In the garden of a rose faery." A devilish grin crept across Willow's lips revealing teeth filed down to points. "Did she tell you her little secret?"

I refused to allow her words to distract me. I tore one of the orbs from my scythe, adjusting my grasp to counter the change in weight.

"Tsk. Tsk. You won't be collecting any souls today."

I felt heat at my back and squatted in just enough time to avoid my head being lopped off by the blade of an ax. "Uh, Clyde. I know you're hurt and all but I could use a little help over here."

I glance over to where Clyde should have been only to discover that I was alone in the gardens. The thought gave me an idea. I hunched down, Willow to my right and another shimmering not so solid figure to my left, though his ax appeared as solid as the ground I stood on. With the entrance to a labyrinth only a few steps behind me, I waited for the perfect opportunity to run for it.

"Now which shall it be? Should I take care of my arch enemy, or collect the soul of poor old Rose?"

"You can't collect her," I said. I saw the parchment. Rose belonged to Clyde.

"My dear naïve wraith. You don't really believe *The Book* would give a collection such as Rose to just one Reaper."

Her comment gave me pause. She called Clyde a Reaper, not a Wraith. "Why do you want her?" I inched back a little, my attention still split between the two entities, though the half-formed one appeared to be consumed with his own thoughts. The thorns of a winding vine poked me in the leg. I was a hair away from the entrance.

"Didn't they tell you?" She tilted her head to the side, a smirk inching across her lips. "Faery are different. They don't go to *The Sands*. And one as old as Rose fetches a pretty penny. Her body will fade, but the dust of her spirit can be used to cultivate beauty in the right hands."

I caught the slight movement behind the half-formed figure, the glittering of an athame my clue that Clyde planned to take care of our phantom the old fashion way. As he eased up behind the entity, he responded to Willow. "Or destroy it. Lavenia Run!"

No need to tell me twice. I risked turning my back and darted into the labyrinth maintaining my lead as I wove a path through the foliage. I swore it reached out to me, slicing my arm, the sharp pains sending me twirling around in circles seeking safety. Who in their right mind builds a labyrinth using roses? With little time to think I allowed a bit of my power to drift outward following the path it chose until I decided I needed a breather. I knew exactly where I was. Though I had not physically visited this place, my power knew it.

"Come out. Come out. Where ever you are?"

She was close. Possibly on the other side of the bush. I dropped to my knees and waited. My ears twitched as I listened intently attempting to discern the sound of footsteps and in which direction she traveled.

Follow your own path. A voice in my head whispered. I inhaled the intoxicating aroma of the flowers and nearly gagged. It was too much. Too many notes of the same fragrance. Returning to shallow breaths, I again reached out. This time I kept my power close following the trail until I reached the center.

"Took you long enough."

There Willow stood, her back to me, the spikes of the mace making up her version of our scythes dripping with a substance I prayed wasn't blood. I summoned my scythe illuminating any darkened corners as I scanned the area hoping if this came down to a fight I didn't have to worry about an extra party intervening.

Her eyes sparkled when she turned to face me. A devious glint, like she knew what I was thinking. "No need to worry about your friend. While I plan to incur the wrath of Nero, I refuse to waste my time and energy playing with toys. Now you. You, my dear, are a worthy adversary completely worth every ounce of my time and attention. I promise to make this as painful as possible."

I allowed her to come for me. Choosing defense first, I gained the opportunity to gauge her strengths and identify any new weaknesses. I already knew of two, one I was sure she would keep under wraps as I'd used it against her before. The other I'd observed when she assumed I was unconscious as she battled Nero. She chose to go low, and I effortlessly avoided the dragging of her mace across the stone ground using my staff as a vaulting pole to clear her and it. The tip of the blade nicked her in the ankle as I swung it around during my descent.

174

She thought she was going to make this painful for me. Let's see how she deals when the tables turn. My scythe only grazed the surface, enough to make her eye the wound in disgust. If only she knew.

She charged again, this time her arm arching, her body twisting as she tried to take my head off only to find that she'd underestimated her target. "Are we really going to continue like this?" I asked, a little bored, a little annoyed.

"This would be so much easier if you'd just die."

Again, I avoided her attack. Lack of patience and planning made her sloppy, a trait ripe for exploitation. I took off through the labyrinth, keeping a few paces ahead of her drawing her into my trap. Her rage fueled the pursuit, making her careless as she cut corners close thorns ripping away skin with each pass. A glance or two over my shoulder just to make sure my pace kept her at a couple of arms-length and I again used my scythe to vault me over the last wall placing me back at the gates leading to the labyrinth. She burst through, the blade of my scythe slicing through her side.

Immediately her hand slapped over the wound as she used her mace to steady herself and stay upright. She considered bolting. I saw the thought cross through her eyes. Doubt also resided there, the uncertainty that she possessed enough strength to escape. On the other side of the garden, Clyde stood, his mid-section bandaged. He leaned against Rose, the leg still not strong enough to fully support his weight.

The air around us grew dark, and I knew what she was trying to do. And try as she might, it made no difference to me. A ripple in time appeared, just big enough for a body to slither through. But she was weak, and it was unstable, and her mind refused to wrap around the idea that she'd officially run out of options.

"This isn't over," she said, stumbling in a futile attempt to move closer to the atmospheric disturbance.

"Oh," I opened my hand palm up revealing my little secret, "I think it is."

Her eyes grew wide at the sight of the hourglass. The cuts she'd sustained earlier at the hands of the roses poured out sand. As the last grain inside the glass made its final descent, I ripped an orb from my scythe, placing it above the hourglass. A scream tore from her throat only to be consumed by the sand filling her body. It was black now. His sand. Nero's sand reclaiming what was once freely given but fractured.

"Willow," my voice held a quiver as her power washed over me, "I return thee to *The Sands*. Reap no more."

I dropped the hourglass into the swirling mist of the orb; it clanked against the sides as it spun like a top before opening and drawing the essence of Willow towards it. Little remained as the last of the black sand siphoned into the orb. A pair of contacts and a charm bracelet. Items unnatural to Nero's world.

Clyde managed to wobble his way over to me. "Where's Rose?" I asked checking behind him.

He held out an orb of his own. The first I'd seen. Now that I thought about it, this was the first time I'd ever seen Clyde reap an entity other than a rogue Reaper. Guess they were right about non-mortal creature's alternative treatment.

I realized then that while I'd collected my bounty, he must have done the same. "What are you going to do with her?"

"She'll go back home." He twirled the orb in his hand, the red dust inside suspended in a vortex. "She may come back. She may not. Not for me to say." He held the parchment in his hand, the edges curling over as they started to burn. He dropped the orb into the center and it sunk away until the last of the parchment ashes blew away in the wind.

I took one last look at the gardens, witnessing their demise since Rose's magic no longer fed them. "This is a nice place. Wonder what will happen to it?" We hopped into the SUV. Well, I hopped, Clyde more like crawled.

"Who knows? She probably willed it to her daughter or like all other abandon places someone will come along and purchase it."

"True." A click of the seatbelt and I turned away. "I'm hungry. How about we make that stop at Angelo's."

Clyde started the engine and pulled out the driveway, "Maybe we should have cleaned up a little?"

I didn't care how I looked. I was tired and hungry, and I'd done just what I needed to do to get me back on track. I was a Wraith and a Reaper, and I was ready to act like one. While my initial focus wasn't on reaping Willow when *The Book* speaks, I too must answer the call.

LANDFALL

BY

MILTON DAVIS

May my words serve as enlightenment to those in darkness and nourishment to those in need. May the knowledge that I share strengthen the foundation that benefits us all.

There was once a man who had a dream, a dream that became a reality, and a reality that became an empire. His name was Cornelius Cassidy, and we are the descendants of his legacy.

-Samake, Cassad Djele/Historian

Cornelius Cassidy emerged from cryosleep in less pain than when he entered. His mouth was extremely dry, his joints ached, but he was anxious for the chamber to open. Ten years after spending a fortune he was finally going to see his dream realized.

"Mr. Cassidy?"

Cornelius's mouth ached when he smiled.

"Dr. Hanes?" he croaked.

"I see you survived. Congratulations."

"I hope that was meant as a joke."

Dr. Hanes laughed, her voice driving the chill from his body.

"So, when do I get to emerge from the crypt?"

"Soon. We're still running vitals. Everything seems to be stable but we have to be sure. We don't often have travelers your age."

"Too young, huh?"

Dr. Hanes laughed again. "If you say so."

Thirty minutes later the chamber opened. Cornelius squinted into the light as two nurses reached in; grasping him gently then lifted him up.

"I can do this myself," he fussed.

"I know, but I'm being safe."

Dr. Hanes appeared, her angelic brown face lifting his spirits. She clamped the exam pad to his wrist then looked at her holo-tablet.

"Vitals are good. You seem to travel well."

"I do a lot of other things well, too," he replied with a wink.

Dr. Hanes rolled her eyes as she smirked. "I'd kill you. Literally."

Cornelius chuckled. "I bet you would."

"Daddy?"

Yvonne Cassidy entered the room. She was the mirror image of her mother at the same age, dusky brown skin with high cheek bones and a dimpled smile.

"Hurry up and get on your suit. You need to see this!"

The nurses fitted him into his bionics. At one hundred and twenty-five he needed the assistance to travel long distances. After a few gestures he sprang to his feet then followed his daughter to the lift which took them to the observation deck. He was greeted by Oyewole Bamidele, ship's captain.

"Mr. Cassidy! Welcome to Cassidy."

The opaque walls turned clear. Cornelius felt as if he was standing in the sky as dense foliage rushed under his feet. Two bare rock columns protruded from the vegetation; in the distance a thunderstorm raged over a grassy plain.

"It's beautiful," he whispered. "Simply beautiful. And it's mine."

"Not quite."

Yuri Yamato strolled onto the deck, looking non-chalant as he gazed down on the planet. The Environ executive exuded the confidence of a man at the top of his game.

"We still have a few papers to sign, Mr. Cassidy."

"You didn't expect me to finalize this deal without inspecting the merchandise, did you?"

Yuri smiled. "Of course not. But this is a bit more than just merchandise, isn't it?"

Cornelius smiled. "Yes, much more. Do you know what this is, Yuri? This is a new start, a second chance, a Final Passage."

Yuri looked confused. "I don't understand."

Cornelius smirked. "Of course, you don't. When can we go planetside?"

"We'll have to wait until the storm passes," Oyewole said. "It's lingering in the vicinity of the compound."

"Your papers will have to wait until then," Cornelius said to Yuri.

The Environ executive walked to stand beside Cornelius. "I have to say you made a fine choice. This one went unnoticed. You're lucky none of the Blocs purchased this first."

"They don't know what to look for," Cornelius said. "Too much money to spend. They've made your company fat with their inefficiency. I estimate their cost overruns exceed 50% of projected costs due to additional terraforming."

"No comment," Yuri answered.

"No need to. I did my homework."

"Yes, you did. The solar deflectors were easy to place and the magnetic field boosters secured the atmosphere much sooner than we anticipated. Accelerated vegetation cycles progressed well and the transplanted fauna adapted rapidly as well."

They fell silent as the storm drifted east.

"Looks like we're ready for landfall," Oyewole said.

"Good," Cornelius replied. "Let's get to the shuttle. I'm ready to put my feet on solid ground."

The team took the lift to the shuttle bay. The shuttle was compact yet comfortable, holding Cornelius, his daughter and Yuri with ease. The craft dropped from the bottom of the ship, falling until it was far enough away to engage engines. It cruised low over the trees, giving a better yet swifter view of the landscape. They dropped low over the grasslands, scattering a herd of wild horses then entered a wide canyon. Cassidy Compound crowned a steep hill rising from the canyon floor, a graceful building promising an interesting tour inside.

"I see you didn't spare any expense," Cornelius groused.

"We treat our best clients like royalty," Yuri said.

"I'd feel better if it wasn't my money you were treating me with."

Yuri laughed. "Believe me, Cornelius; we threw this in pro bono."

"We'll see," Cornelius answered.

The shuttle came to a gentle rest on the upper landing pad. Cornelius stepped outside then took a deep breath. The air was sweeter than the ship, with a tinge of an organic smell that meant new life.

"This is pure air," Yuri commented. "I love the way a new world smells. Or should I say how it doesn't smell. Remember this moment, Mr. Cassidy. It goes downhill from here."

"Not if I can help it," Cornelius whispered.

"Shall we go inside?" Yuri said.

"Not yet." Cornelius took a moment longer to gaze on his gamble. If not one person ever migrated to Cassidy he would still feel successful.

"Okay, let's go inside."

Yuri led them through the functional structure to the main conference room. They spread out around the table as an Environ employee served them glasses of water.

Cornelius took a sip then grinned. "The water is as good as the air."

"Our work is first rate. It also helps when the heavenly body responds well to our handling."

Yuri's eyes studied Yvonne as he spoke.

"Let's get down to business," Cornelius said. "What do we have here?"

Yuri stood then activated the controls for the holoscreen. An image of Cassidy appears, spinning slowly on its axis.

"What we have is a class M-2 planet orbiting a G2V star. Our distance from the star is approximately 85 percent that of Earth, hence the solar defectors. Currently the temperature patterns are tropical to subtropical, but we are forming ice capes both north and south. The equatorial region is currently uninhabitable due to extreme heat but we expect that to moderate over the next twenty years."

"It there any chance the ice capes will expand to glaciers?" Yvonne asked.

"No," Yuri replied. "We provide climate monitoring at no charge for the next two hundred years. It usually takes that long for weather patterns to establish themselves."

The planet view zoomed in as Yuri approached the image.

"We've designated 30 initial sites for prime city development. We expect another 15 to come online once the patterns settle. For now, there is no threat of volcanic activity or earthquakes."

Cornelius eyebrow rose. "For now?"

"We're working on establishing a molten core," Yuri said. "It helps to anchor the atmosphere if the planet can generate its own magnetic field and a molten core is essential for it."

"I'm not sure I like that," Cornelius said.

"It's a necessary evil for a class M planet."

"How soon before we can start settling people," Yvonne asked.

"A year from now," Yuri replied. "How are your recruitment efforts going?"

Cornelius sagged in his seat. "Not good. So far, we have 750,000 signed. We'll probably lose half of those once we begin boarding on the ark ships."

For the first time since landfall Yuri looked displeased. "Our agreement called on an initial payment then a 100-year lease based on planet production. You'll need at least one million people to meet our requirements."

Cornelius took on a hard look. "Yvonne?"

His daughter handed Yuri a bank tablet. The screen displayed the Environ/Cassidy transaction data.

"Press enter," she said.

Yuri pressed enter. The remaining balance for Cassidy appeared in the Environ account.

"Oh my God!" Yuri whispered.

"You can verify it if you like. I think our business with Environ is done."

"Yes, I think it is."

"Can you deliver the other documents so we can make this deal final?"

Yuri was almost giddy. "Yes, I can. It will take a moment to download them."

Yvonne sat close to Cornelius.

"It's all yours now, daddy," she whispered.

"Yes, it is, baby girl."

"And we are now officially flat broke," she added.

"For now," he replied. "I've been here before. Don't I always rise again?"

Yvonne kissed his cheek. "Like a phoenix, daddy. Just like a phoenix."

* * *

Thomas Cassidy slumped in his office chair then moaned when he read the intertex from his sister. His forehead furrowed as he read the text again, hoping he'd got it wrong. But he hadn't. He pushed away from his mahogany desk then trudged to the window wall, looking down on the busy Atlanta streets. For the last 20 years he'd worked hard help-ing his father build Cassidy Enterprises into the most powerful company in the world. Now it was all gone, just like that.

He tapped his ear then waited for his mother to answer.

"Hello, Tommy," she said.

Her mellow voice eased his anger.

"Mamma, he did it."

There was silence for a moment.

"Tommy, I want you to close the office and come to the house right now. We have some things to discuss."

"We can talk right now," Tommy answered.

"Don't get fussy with me, boy," she replied sternly. "You come on down. I'll be in the garden."

"I might as well," he said. "It's not like we're solvent or anything."

"Quit sassing and come down," she said.

"Yes, mama."

Thomas sent a broadcast text to the office employees then cringed as a collective whoop went up. People hurried from their desk in a jubilant exodus to the elevators. He knew he wasn't as well liked as his father. He was considered a task master, which he was. Someone had to make up for all the money his father was spending lately. And now that he knew the reason he wouldn't be any better.

His personal sped him to the south Metro area to the house. "House" was an understatement; the Cassidy compound was a 2000-acre wooded nature preserve. The massive gate identified his personal and the gate opened. The small vehicle entered, proceeding up the paved driveway to the mansion. The driveway ended at the cul-de-sac; the personal stopped then Thomas jumped out, fast walking to the back of house. Mamma was tending her vegetable garden as always, wearing her dirty coveralls and large plantation hat. She looked up with her big smile, her smooth sepia face hiding her almost ninety years of life.

"Mamma, what's going on?" Thomas blurted.

"Give me a kiss, boy," she replied. "I ain't seen you all day."

Thomas rolled his eyes then kissed her on the cheek.

"You smell like earthworms," he said.

Mamma chuckled. "So, what's this about us being broke?"

"Daddy paid off the balance on Cassidy," he said. "He cleaned us out!"

Mamma walked away to her tomatoes. "All of it?"

"All of it."

She pushed back her hat. "I thought he would. No sense leaving things undone."

"What are you talking about?"

"Go get me my chair," she said.

Thomas hurried to the shed then brought back her folding chair. Mamma sat hard then wiped her brow.

"You know your daddy is dying, right?" she said.

Thomas looked solemn. "I know he's not in the best of health but..."

Mamma reached out then took his trembling hand. "No, son your daddy is dying. Soon. It's why he went to Cassidy and why he paid off the balance. He didn't want to leave us in debt."

"So, he's leaving us broke?"

Mamma smiled. "Cornelius spent all his money. He ain't spent any of mine."

Thomas was startled. "Your money?"

Mamma nodded. "Me and Cornelius always kept our money separate. Just in case he got in trouble."

Thomas cleared his throat. "Mamma if you don't mind me asking; how much money do you have?"

Mamma's eyes narrowed. "I ain't never told your daddy. Why you think I'm going to tell you? Let's just say I have enough to see things through."

She stood up then waved Thomas close.

"Come on. Let's walk to the house. We have some things to do."

* * *

Yuri grinned at the father and daughter.

"That seems to conclude our business," he said. "It' been a pleasure working with you."

Cornelius's smiled faded. "I don't think we're quite done yet, Yuri."

The Environ rep forced a smile. "Is there something else?"

"I believe there is," Cornelius replied. "A matter of something on 'my' planet that doesn't belong to me."

"What are you talking about?" Yuri maintained a rigid smile.

"Don't make me do this," Cornelius warned.

Yuri seemed dumbfounded, but Cornelius knew better.

"Let's take another ride," he said.

The trio returned to the main ship.

"Wole," Yvonne said. "Take us to the other site."

Oyewole nodded then the ship sped off. Yuri pulled at his collar.

"I don't see what this is all about."

Cornelius didn't reply. They streaked over a long stretch of forest before coming across a mountain range. Oyewole weaved the ship through the narrow passages until another building appeared.

"Ever seen that place before?" Cornelius asked Yuri.

"I can't say that I have," Yuri replied.

"I can say one thing about you. You stick to a lie until the end. It's an Environ monitoring station. It's got everything you need to keep close tabs on planet development. It also contains a big dose of

Environ security tech just in case things don't go the way you planned."

"Cornelius, I had no idea..."

"Maybe you didn't, maybe you did. That doesn't matter. What matters is that this is my planet now and I want it gone."

"Just supposing this does belong to Environ. It would take years to dismantle and remove such a complex structure."

"Then I'll let you lease the land and tax your services until you can remove it," Cornelius said.

"You can't do that!"

"Yes, I can. It's my planet now and you're trespassing. An incident like this would give the Blocs just the evidence they need to extend government control over your operations."

Yuri dropped his act. "They couldn't if they tried."

"You're correct, but they'll try. Environ doesn't need the distraction. You have worlds to build."

"So, what do you propose?" Yuri asked.

"The deal I just offered."

"I'll contact my office," Yuri said. "You'll have an answer in the morning."

He stalked away to his cabin.

"Good work, Yvonne," Cornelius said. "Looks like we're not so broke after all."

Yvonne smiled. "I'll contact mamma and Tommy."

"Please do. That boy is probably pulling his hair out right about now."

Yvonne laughed. "Like father like son."

Cornelius smiled. "Unfortunately, true. But once he comes he'll change his mind. Too bad I won't be alive to see it."

Yvonne's smile faded. She walked away to carry out her duties.

Oyewole steered the ship away from the Environ facility.

Cornelius gazed at the pristine landscape, fighting a feeling of melancholy.

"Not much time left," he whispered. "None at all."

* * *

Thomas flinched from pain in his right thigh. He looked over at his mother, a frown on her face. He blinked his eyes then turned his attention to Reverend Charles Roy as he reached the climax of his stirring sermon. Half the congregation stood on their feet, shouting amen and holding up their hands in agreement and worship. Thomas almost rolled his eyes but remembered the painful pinch to his thigh just a moment ago. I swear that woman still thinks I'm eight, he thought.

"Get ready," mamma said. "You're up soon."

He couldn't believe he agreed to this. The fate of Cassidy Enterprises hung in the balance despite mamma's cash infusion and he was about to deliver a speech, the most important speech in his life if mamma was to be believed. But Thomas was never much on faith. His constant mantra was 'faith had nothing to do with it.' But it was mamma's money, so she made the rules. For now.

He suffered through five more minutes of sermonizing, the opening of the church doors then the obligatory collecting of the tithes. He was about to let the plate pass him by when mamma elbowed his ribs. He reluctantly dropped a twenty in the plate. Mamma gave much more, frowning at him all the while.

"We might need that money tomorrow," he whispered.

"Be quiet, boy. Your time is coming up."

After a few brief announcements by Bessie Lansbury, the church secretary, Reverend Charles took to the pulpit again.

"The Lord has blessed us with a good word today and I know y'all are ready to go home. But before we dismiss I seek your patience for a little bit longer. Cornelius Cassidy's boy, Thomas, has a few words to deliver on behalf of his father."

Reverend Charles turned to him. "Thomas?"

Thomas straightened his tie then took the podium. He looked out into the sanctuary and a hard knot formed in his stomach. He couldn't do this. He knew most everyone sitting before him. These were people that nurtured him from when he was a boy. To tell them what he was about to tell them, to convince these people who were like a second family to do what he proposed he had to believe it was the right thing to do. And that was the problem.

"Thank you, Reverend Charles. I'm not going to hold everyone long. I'm here to deliver a simple message and offer a life changing opportunity. A few days ago, my father accomplished a lifelong dream. He purchased a planet."

The sanctuary erupted in applause. Thomas waited until silence settled in the room again before speaking.

"But what's a world without people? My father is many things, but he's not The Almighty."

Laughter broke the tension and eased Thomas's mind.

"I come today to ask some of you to make a special commitment; a life changing commitment. Thousands of miles and five years away is a world

waiting to be filled. It's a world ripe with new op-
portunities and it's waiting for you. Yes you. We are
willing to transport anyone wishing to build a new
future to our planet. We have ten ark ships waiting
to take all of you who are willing to a new life, a life
which all of us deserve without any restrictions. I
know this is not for everyone. This is a one-way
journey. You'll never see Earth again. But this is
also the opportunity of a lifetime. A chance to build
a society where second class does not apply, where
racism doesn't exist. A chance to build a truly equal
society. I would say more, but I'm not going to sell
you. The opportunity speaks for itself. I appreciate
your attention and I hope you think long and hard
about this opportunity."

Thomas went back to his seat to modest applause. The congregation looked confused mostly.

"That was terrible," he whispered.

"You did just fine," mamma said. "Short and
straightforward, just like your daddy."

Reverend Charles took the podium again.

"Thank you, Thomas. Your father is a good
friend, a good deacon and a good brother. I hope
everyone here today takes the time to consider this
opportunity. Remember wherever God's people go,
so shall He be. I'd also like to let everyone here
know that when those ark ships lift off to Cassidy,
I'll be one of the passengers."

Thomas gasped with the congregation.

"I told you it was going to work out," Mamma
whispered.

* * *

Cornelius sat in the prep room of the ship, his
daughter holding his hand. He looked at her nervous smile then patted her hand.

"Look at you. You'd think that you're the one going under the knife."

"Don't say that," Yvonne replied. "It sounds so terrible."

"So squeamish, just like your mother. Speaking of her, have you heard any word from them?"

"Their almost home," Yvonne said. "50,000 away from full capacity."

"Good, good. Looks like we have ourselves a viable planet."

"Not quite," Yvonne said. "Mamma said they're going to have to go abroad to get the last 50,000."

Cornelius pouted. "I was afraid of that. But they can do it. Thomas is a good son. He'll get it done whether he wants to or not."

Dr. Hanes entered the room with her usual bright smile.

"So, are you ready, Mr. Cassidy?"

"Ready as I'll ever be."

Dr. Hanes put the analysis band on his wrist then scanned the table. When she looked up her face was serious.

"You know we don't have to do this, don't you? There's technology that can perform the same function and be nowhere near as intrusive."

"I want this," he said. "We're making history and I want every bit of it recorded. Every bit."

Dr. Hanes looked at Yvonne. "Any chance we can bully him out of this?"

"I'm afraid not," Yvonne answered.

"Let me put it this way, Cornelius; this is a stressful operation. You could die."

"I'm already dying, Zarina. A lot faster than most. So, let's get this over with. We've missed too much already."

"Okay, then let's get started."

Dr. Hanes and Yvonne left the room. They activated the sealing sequence then initiated sterilization mode as she linked into the surgical robotics.

"How does this work again, Doctor?" Yvonne asked.

The Djele implant will be embedded into the cerebral cortex. Once it's in place a stimulant will be injected and the unit will merge with his brain. Its outer layer was constructed from your father's protein structure so there is no chance for rejection. From that point on it will record everything your father experiences. It will also enhance his memory."

Yvonne looked at her father lying on the operating table, surrounded by the surgery robots.

"And when he dies?"

"The unit will be removed. The data will be harvested for future reference."

Dr. Hanes performed a few preliminary motions to confirm complete synchronicity. A bot moved closer to her father then attached an IV filled with anesthesia. Yvonne could see her father's body relax.

"We're ready to proceed. Are you ready Yvonne?"

Yvonne cleared her throat. "Yes I am."

"Okay then. Here we go."

Yvonne said a prayer as Dr. Hanes made the first incision.

* * *

Thomas took off his jacket, rolled up his sleeves then loosened his tie as he gazed at the rows of sailboats in Durban mooring. He fidgeted as he waited for his contact, unhappy with the world. There was something strange about summer weather in

December. He didn't care what hemisphere he was in, it just wasn't right. He wondered what odd conditions he would face on Cassidy, what strange weather patterns would set off his allergies after spending all that money to get them under control. So, when Angelica Buthelezi strode to his table with her statuesque looks and glowing smile he was not swayed.

"You're late," he said.

Angelica sat before him then took off her shades. "Good afternoon to you too, Thomas."

"So, what's the verdict?"

Angelica raised her palm to Thomas's face with a frown.

"Angelica, I don't have time for..."

"Silence," she commanded. "First things first."

A waiter glided to the table.

"Welcome, Ms. Buthelezi," he crooned. "Shall I bring you your wine?"

"Yes, Baxter, and bless you for remembering."

Baxter grinned. "How could I forget?"

The waiter glided away. Angelica leaned back in her seat.

"I'll have 30,000 ready in two weeks," she said.

"Thirty? That's all?" Thomas rubbed his head. "That's twenty thousand short."

"It's the best I can do with such short notice," Angelica replied. "Besides this is illegal. If the AU discovered what we're doing we'll both be thrown in prison."

"You think I don't know that?" Thomas wiped his sweaty forehead with a napkin, and then pulled a handful of rand from his pocket.

"You're leaving?" Angelica said.

"Of course, I am. I need to find 20,000 more people to take this trip, and I won't find them sipping wine and staring at your breasts."

Angelica smiled. "So, you did notice."

Thomas managed to smile. "Of course, I did."

The waiter arrived with Angelica's wine. She took a sip then nodded in approval.

"They'll be ready in two weeks," she said. "I've arranged a rendezvous in Natal."

"Make sure everyone is there and ready to go. We'll have a short window."

Angelica took another sip. "Don't worry. You should try Congo."

"For what?"

"For your other 20,000. Things are still unsettled there. You'll find plenty people willing to leave."

"But will they be the right people?" Thomas asked.

"Beggars can't be choosers." Angelica went into her purse then took out a Graycell™.

"Look at this when you're alone. He's a good contact."

Thomas took the chip then put it in his wallet. Angelica turned up her cheek; Thomas sighed then kissed it.

"We used to have so much fun," she said. "I miss the old Thomas."

"I miss him too," Thomas replied. "Goodbye, Angelica."

Thomas strode out the club to a waiting limo. One more stop then he was done.

"I hope you appreciate what I'm doing here, old man," he whispered. "I damn sure hope you do."

    *   *   *

The ship followed the winding river, swaying with the turns. Cornelius stood before the window flanked by Yvonne and Dr. Haynes, his arms folded behind his back. Bandages still covered his head from the surgery, but he insisted that they take this trip as soon as possible. The doctor monitored his vital signs, the holoscreen hovering before her eyes.

"There," he said. "Do you see it?"

Yvonne nodded. "Yes, I see it."

The doctor glanced from the screen. "It's beautiful. You should sit down."

Cornelius gave her a sidelong glance. "I'll sit when I'm ready. Take us down closer."

The ship descended giving a better view of island.

"That's it. That's where I want to be buried," Cornelius said.

Yvonne was visibly upset. "That's why you brought us here? To show us where you want to be buried?"

Cornelius gave Yvonne a stern look. "Yes."

"The transports from Earth are arriving soon," she said. "We don't have time for this."

"Then make time!" The sudden emotion triggered a sharp pain in his head. Cornelius reached out then found his chair. He sat down hard. Yvonne was immediately at his side.

"Doctor?"

Dr. Haynes studied his scans. "He's still healing. The implant is still syncing. You'll have to keep your conversations friendly for now."

Cornelius waved Yvonne away.

"You're right. There are more serious things to attend to. I needed you to know just in case your mother wasn't able to..."

"She'll come, daddy," Yvonne assured him. "I don't know about Thomas, but I know mama will come."

"I hope so. I did this for her, too."

"Let get back to main base," Yvonne said. "We're the welcoming committee, remember?"

* * *

Ten huge transports circled Cassidy, each pregnant with 100,000 anxious passengers. The journey through the gates had been traumatic, especially for those who'd never experience jump space, which was most of them. No sooner had the ships established orbit did they begin filling the shuttles to take everyone planetside. A steady stream of the smaller ships descended single file through space then atmosphere, guided by skilled Environ controllers.

Cornelius watched the first shuttle touch down on the tarmac. Tears came to his eyes, as they did to Yvonne and even Dr. Haynes.

"Damn it, I hate crying," the doctor said. "But this is so beautiful. You must be so proud, Cornelius."

"You have no idea how much," Cornelius replied, his voice cracking.

The terminal could have been designed to release the passengers inside as was the norm, but Cornelius wanted each new resident to experience Cassidy as soon as possible. The ship taxied to fifty yards of them then came to a complete stop. The doors lifted then the stairway extended to the asphalt. The first to emerge was a young family; a husband, wife, two children and one infant. The report said the infant was born during transport, making her one of the first true citizens of Cassidy.

Two stewards guided the bewildered family to Cornelius and the others. Cornelius greeted them with a magnanimous smile. He shook the young father's hand then hugged his wife and children. This is what it was about, creating a new life for the young ones.

"Welcome to Cassidy," he said. "Welcome home."

Thomas took a long drag from his cigar then placed it on the holder beside the holobar on his coffee table. He glanced outside for a moment, savoring the Atlanta skyline. This was home. This right here. No matter what he was told, this was where he was meant to be.

The Environ technician had come earlier that day to install the bar. It was secret technology; he was not to let anyone know he possessed it. He had a mind to whisk it away to his R&D department to 'receive and duplicate' but he didn't want to cause trouble for anyone else. He'd done enough of that already.

He was officially banned from the African Continent by the AU for participating in illegal immigration. The company's assets had been seized and extradition orders filed with the US. But Thomas was a pro at getting in and getting out of trouble. As long as he stayed away from the continent he'd be fine. He had no intentions of going back. He had no intentions of going anywhere.

A piercing sound like the netline warning system filled the room. A blue light emerged from the Environ bar, halting about 12 inches above the device. A face appeared, an attractive female with red hair and freckles.

"Thomas Cassidy?" The woman said.

"That's me. And you are..."

"Catlyn Rogers, Environ Communications specialist. Please stand by."

The woman's face disappeared, replace by a 3D image of Yvonne.

"Vonne!"

"Hi Tommy!" Yvonne waved at him like a child. "It's so good to see you!"

"Same here. How is everyone?"

"They're good. Mama asked if you were keeping up her garden."

"Of course," Thomas lied.

Yvonne smirked. "Who did you hire?"

"Seasonal Landscapes," he answered. "You know I hate dirt."

They both laughed harder than they should have.

"How is everything?" Thomas finally asked.

"I can't imagine how it could be better," Yvonne answered. "We're keeping the settlers contained at the Environ cities for now while we begin construction on new cities. The planet is terraformed but there are still a few restricted areas."

"And how's daddy doing?"

"He's great. The change has done wonders for him."

And momma?

Yvonne chuckled. "Starting a new garden and bossing daddy around. The only thing missing is you."

Thomas slumped into his chair then picked up his cigar.

"Don't start, Vonne."

"Tommy, please come. We miss you and we're a family. You should be here with us."

"I'm a grown ass man," Thomas snapped. "I should be where I want to be."

"You're afraid," Yvonne said. "I know you are."

"Whether I am or not doesn't matter," he said. "I'm staying here."

"This is a new future, Tommy. A dream come true."

"I'm not a dreamer, Vonne. You know that. Besides, someone has to run the store."

"We don't need the store anymore. We have everything we need right here."

They were silent for a moment. Yvonne was right; he was afraid. It's one thing to go live in another country, but another planet? One built by human hands? Too many things could go wrong. He did miss his family, but not enough to make such a drastic change.

"I'm glad y'all are happy. I really am. But I can't come, Vonne. I can't."

Yvonne sighed. "Daddy said you wouldn't. This time I wanted him to be wrong. He wanted me to tell you that as of today Cassidy Enterprises, LLC belongs to you. You'll receive the paperwork within the week."

"Everything? To me?"

Yvonne nodded. "He's cutting ties completely."

Thomas put down the cigar. "Tell him I said thank you."

"You could tell him yourself," Yvonne said.

"No, it's best you did. We would only end up arguing."

Yvonne's eyes glistened. "Goodbye, Tommy. I love you."

Thomas felt a tear running down his cheek. "Goodbye Vonne. Love you, too."

Yvonne's image faded. The blue light descended into the bar then blinked out.

Thomas wiped his eyes as he sauntered to the window. So that was it. Just like that. It all belonged to him now. He looked out onto the city, the highway filled with traffic, jets filing into and flying out of Hartsfield like an airborne merry-go-round. Up there, out there somewhere his family was starting a new life without him. He never felt so alone in his life.

* * *

The ship cruised over the northern polar region, its third flyover in two days. The pilot checked her fuel reading then glanced at her solitary passenger. She was well aware of whom he was but it didn't make her job any easier. At some point the overtime didn't matter. She wanted to go home to her family.

"Seen enough?" she said, hoping her irritation didn't come across in her voice.

Thomas puffed his cigar.

"Yeah, I guess so. Can't avoid it any longer. Take me to Cassidy,"

The pilot grinned as she changed course south. Three hours later they cruised over the capital city. Thomas marveled at how normal it looked. He expected something different, better maybe. Though the cities were a disappointment, the planet was amazing. Yvonne was right. He should have come long ago.

The ship landed on the Cassidy compound pad. He was barely out of it when Yvonne rushed up to him and almost knocked him down as she hugged him.

"I'm so happy to see you, Tommy!" she said.

Thomas hugged her tight and let the tears flow.

"Looks like I'm home," he said.

Yvonne took his hand. "Let's get you settled."

"Not yet. I want to see them first."

Yvonne's smile faded. "You sure?"

Thomas wiped his eyes. "Yes. I'm sure."

They boarded a small shuttle then flew to the island. Thomas's eyes glistened as the mausoleum came into focus. He should have come sooner. His fear and selfishness kept him away. He had to watch both of them pass away in the holofeeds after awakening from cryosleep.

The shuttle landed near the entrance. Thomas followed Yvonne inside; he grinned when he saw the garden surrounding their tombs. There was bench opposite the tombs; Thomas sat down then folded his hands on his lap. Yvonne sat beside him.

"Now what?" he said.

"Now we run a planet," Yvonne said.

"This isn't like running a corporation," Thomas said. "We have to make laws, establish court systems, and maybe even fight wars. There's a planet grab happening as we speak. We might get caught in the middle of it."

"Daddy thought of that," Yvonne said. "We're way off the normal jump routes. We're also totally self-sufficient, unlike the other terraformed planets. By the time they find us, we'll be more than ready."

Thomas looked at Yvonne and smiled. She was so confident, but that was her way. She was just like Daddy that way.

"Are you sure about that?"

"I am, now that you're here," she said.

Thomas hugged her.

"Let's go then."

"So soon?" Yvonne said.

"I can always come back. The sooner we start the better. We have a world to run."

They stood then held hands as they left the gardens, both of them glancing back at the twin tombs. They wouldn't fail them. They couldn't.

* * *

The pilot circled the sacred island awaiting orders. Ziara Harriet Nzinga Cassad gazed down on the monument, a smile on her handsome yet stern face. So long she'd waited for this moment and now it was before her. It was a glorious time indeed.

"Take us down," she ordered.

The armed shuttle plunged through the clouds to the landing pad. Ziara was standing at the port before it touched down flanked by two Royal guardsmen, their red armor in sharp contrast to her black body hugging suit. A Cassad kente cloak hung from her shoulders matching the elaborate head wrap holding her flowing dreads in place. They strode from the shuttle as soon as the doors opened. What was once a small mausoleum was now the grand building it deserved to be. The guards snapped to attention as the trio entered the pyramid shaped structure. They crossed the expanded garden to the four tombs in the center. Ziara raised her hand and they halted.

She extended her left hand. The guard on her left handed her a gilded box. She took the box then walked to the tomb of the Matriarch. She opened the box, revealing a small shovel and seeds. Ziara knelt then dug a shallow hole in the rich soil. She placed the seeds into the hole then covered it.

She ambled back to the guards then extended her right hand. The other guard handed her a narrow wooden box. She took the box then sat on the bench before the tombs, the original bench Yvonne and Thomas Cassidy sat over five hundred years ago as they lay the foundation of what would become the Cassad Empire. She opened the box then took out the cigar and lighter. She placed the cigar in her mouth then lit it as she had practiced numerous times. The smoke did not choke her as it did her first time. She actually grew to like the custom, although she rarely indulged.

She took her time, smoking the entire cigar. After she finished she stood then bowed deeply.

"Thank you, ancestors, for what you have given us," she said. "Thank you for your vision. Thank you for your bloodline. I hope I do not shame you."

She turned then marched for the shuttle, the guardsmen falling in step. The shuttle waited, the port door open. Ziara settled into her seat.

"Take us up," she commanded.

The shuttle lifted then streaked upward through the clouds then out of the atmosphere into space. Ziara smiled as the war fleet came into view. Cornelius Cassidy had the foresight to create a planet away from the traffic of the other worlds, giving Cassad ample time to grow, develop and prosper. Because of his vision the planet suffered the least during the Dark Age and was the first to emerge from those terrible times. Now it was time for Cassad to take its rightful place, a light of hope among the devastation.

"Open the comm," she said.

She waited until the clear signal registered in her comm.

"Five hundred years we've waited," she said, her voice echoing in every ship. "Now is our opportunity to show our ancestors the honor they rightly deserve. Now is the time for us to claim what is ours. I expect the best of each and every one of you. Don't disappoint them. Most of all do not disappoint me. Ago!"

"Ame!"

Ziara leaned back into her chair, the faces of her baloguns appearing before her.

"Where do we go first?" Balogun Ojetade asked.

"Where it all began," she said.

BLACKTASTIC! BIOS

Linda Addison
Linda Addison born in Philadelphia, PA is an American poet and writer of horror, fantasy, and science fiction. Addison is the first African-American winner of the HWA Bram Stoker Award®, which she won four times for her collections Consumed, Reduced to Beautiful Grey Ashes (2001) and Being Full of Light, Insubstantial (2007) and How To Recognize A Demon Has Become Your Friend (2011) and Four Elements (2014). Linda was recently announced the winner of the the Horror Writers Association Lifetime Achievement Award.

Sheree Renée Thomas
Sheree Renée Thomas is the author of Sleeping Under the Tree of Life (Aqueduct Press, named on the 2016 James Tiptree, Jr. Award "Worthy" List and honored with a Publishers Weekly Starred Review) and Shotgun Lullabies: Stories & Poems. She is the editor of the groundbreaking anthologies, Dark Matter: A Century of Speculative Fiction from the African Diaspora (winner of the 2001 World Fantasy Award) and Dark Matter: Reading the Bones (winner of the 2005 World Fantasy Award).

Her speculative stories and poems also appear in Apex Magazine, Harvard's Transition, Smith's Meridians, NYU's Black Renaissance Noire, Callaloo, ESSENCE, So Long Been Dreaming:

Postcolonial Science Fiction & Fantasy, Mythic Delirium, Strange Horizons, Revise the Psalm: Writers Celebrate the Work of Gwendolyn Brooks, The Moment of Change: An Anthology of Feminist Speculative Poetry, An Alphabet of Embers: An Anthology of Unclassiafiables, Jalada Afrofuture(s), Afrofuturo(s), Stories for Chip: A Tribute to Samuel R. Delany, Inks Crawl, Memphis Noir, Mojo Rising: Contemporary Writers, and the black women's horror anthology, Sycorax's Daughters.

Her work has been translated in French, Urdu, and Spanish and her essays, articles, and reviews have appeared in the New York Times and other publications. Based in Memphis, Tennessee, Thomas is the Associate Editor of Obsidian: Literature in the African Diaspora.

Nicole Kurtz

Nicole Givens Kurtz's short stories have appeared in over 25 anthologies of science fiction, fantasy, and horror. Her novels have been finalists for the EPPIEs, Dream Realm, and Fresh Voices in science fiction awards. Her work has appeared in Stoker Finalist, Sycorax's Daughters, and in such professional anthologies as Baen's Straight Outta Tombstone and Onyx Path's The Endless Ages Anthology.

Valjeanne Jeffers

Valjeanne Jeffers is a speculative fiction author, a graduate of Spelman College and the author of ten books: including her Immortal series, and her most recent Mona Livelong: Paranormal Dectective series. Her first novel, Immortal, is featured on the Invisible Universe Documentary time-line. She was also choosen as a Seer (2016) by the Horror Writers Association (HWA).

Her writing has been published in numerous anthologies including: The City: A Cyberfunk Anthology; Steamfunk!; Genesis Science Fiction Magazine; The Ringing Ear: Black Poets Lean South (as Valjeanne Jeffers-Thompson); Griots: A Sword and Soul Anthology; Liberated Muse I: How I Freed My Soul; PurpleMag; Drumvoices Revue; Griots II: Sisters of the Spear; Possibilities; Say it Loud; Black Gold and, most recently, Luminescent Threads: Connections to Octavia E. Butler; Fitting In; Sycorax's Daughters (which has been nominated for the Bram Stoker Award); 100 Black Women in Horror and Black Magic Women.

Valjeanne is also one of the screen writers for the horror anthology film, 7Magpies (in production).

Kenesha Williams

Kenesha Williams is an independent author, speaker, and Founder/Editor-in-Chief of Black Girl Magic Literary Magazine. She took to heart the advice, "If you don't see a clear path for what you want, sometimes you have to make it yourself," and created a speculative fiction literary magazine featuring characters that were representative of the diversity of Black womanhood. She has happily parlayed her love for the weird and the macabre into Black Girl Magic Literary Magazine, finding the best in undiscovered talent in Speculative Fiction. A gifted communicator, Kenesha has been a panelist and speaker at many conferences and events, as well as a guest on several podcasts. As an essayist she has written for Time Magazine imprint Motto. Kenesha is also a screenwriter who is in preproduction on a horror genre web series and a short horror film. When she has free time, she spends it reading, writing, or using all her iPhone memory listening to a million podcasts. She currently lives in the DC Metro Area with her husband and three little boys.

Balogun Ojetade

As Technical Director of the Afrikan Martial Arts Institute and Co-Chair of the Urban Survival and Preparedness Institute, Balogun Ojetade is the author of the bestselling non-fiction books *Afrikan Martial Arts: Discovering the Warrior Within, The Afrikan Warriors Bible, Surviving the Urban Apocalypse, The Urban Self Defense Manual, The Young Afrikan Warriors' Guide to Defeating Bullies & Trolls, Never Unarmed: The Afrikan Warriors' Guide to Improvised Weapons, Ofo Ase: 365 Daily Affirmations to Awaken the Afrikan Warrior Within, Ori: The Afrikan Warriors' Mindset* and *Ogun Ye! Protecting the Afrikan Family and Community*.

He is one of the leading authorities on Afroretroism – film, fashion or fiction that combines African and / or African American culture with a blend of "retro" styles and futuristic technology, in order to explore the themes of tension between past and future and between the alienating and empowering effects of technology and on Creative Resistance. He writes about Afroretroism – Sword & Soul, Rococoa, Steamfunk and Dieselfunk at http://chroniclesofharriet.com/.

He is author of eighteen novels and gamebooks – *MOSES: The Chronicles of Harriet Tubman (Books 1 & 2); The Chronicles of Harriet Tubman:*

Freedonia; *Redeemer*; *Once Upon A Time In Afrika*; *Fist of Afrika*; *A Single Link*; *Wrath of the Siafu*; *The Scythe*; *The Keys*; *Redeemer: The Cross Chronicles*; *Beneath the Shining Jewel*; *Q-T-Pies: The Savannah Swan Files (Book 0)* and *A Haunting in the SWATS: The Savannah Swan Files (Book 1)*; *Siafu Saves the World*; *Siafu vs. The Horde; Dembo's Ditty*; and *The Beatdown* – contributing co-editor of three anthologies: *Ki:Khanga: The Anthology*, *Steamfunk* and *Dieselfunk* and contributing editor of the *Rococoa* anthology and *Black Power: The Superhero Anthology*.

He is also the creator and author of the Afrofuturistic manga series, *Jagunjagun Lewa (Pretty Warrior)* and co-author of the *Ngolo* graphic novel.

Finally, he is co-author of the award winning screenplay, *Ngolo* and co-creator of *Ki Khanga: The Sword and Soul Role-Playing Game*, both with author Milton Davis.

Kyoko M

Kyoko M is a USA Today bestselling author, a fangirl, and an avid book reader. She has a Bachelor of Arts in English Lit degree from the University of Georgia, which gave her every valid excuse to devour book after book with a concentration in Greek mythology and Christian mythology. When not working feverishly on a manuscript (or two), she can be found buried under her Dashboard on Tumblr, or chatting with fellow nerds on Twitter, or curled up with a good Harry Dresden novel on a warm Georgia night. Like any author, she wants nothing more than to contribute something great to the best profession in the world, no matter how small.

Marcus Haynes

M. Haynes' childhood was so filled with fantasy worlds that he just had to create one of his own. This Memphis-born, Mississippi-bred son of the South was inspired all through his upbringing by books like Harry Potter and Animorphs, TV shows like Avatar the Last Airbender, and video games like Legend of Dragoon to start writing, a passion he has continued to adulthood. His YA science fantasy the Elemental series and his other writings take a different turn from most of his childhood fantasy worlds, however. Armed with over fifteen years of writing experience, M. Haynes has set out to produce works that show that you don't have to be a straight, blonde haired, blue eyed guy to be a superhero. Instead, he hopes to show a more nuanced version of people of color in fantasy worlds, maybe even encouraging young P.O.C. to love reading and writing as he does. You can learn more about M. Haynes and his work at www.mhaynes.org/elemental.

Alan Jones

Amazon Best-selling author & former Wall Street consultant, Alan Jones was born and raised in Atlanta, GA. He has three Sci-Fi books under his belt, *To Wrestle with Darkness, Sacrifices* and his latest, *Heretics.* Alan has also contributed to a number of Anthologies, such as "The City: A *CyberFunk Anthology*", *Possibilities*& the soon to be released *Terminus.* Alan was formerly a columnist with the Atlanta Tribune, as well being a movie reviewer for *The Technique* &*The Signal* during his college days. When not writing, Alan works as an Oracle Consultant.

Alan attended Georgia Tech and the Robinson School of Business, obtaining his MBA from the latter. www.Alandjones.com

Violette Meier

Violette Meier is a happily married mother, writer, painter, poet, and native of Atlanta, Georgia, who earned my B.A. in English at Clark Atlanta University and a Masters of Divinity at Interdenominational Theological Center.

Her books include: *The First Chronicle of Zayashariya: Out of Night, Angel Crush, Son of the Rock, Tales of a Numinous Nature: A Short Story Collection, Violette Ardor: A Volume of Poetry,* and *This Sickness We Call Love: Poems of Love, Lust, and Lamentation, Ruah the Immortal,* and *Loving and Living Life* are now available.

Aziza Sphinx

Aziza Sphinx is a firm believer that reading and writing go hand and hand. A Southerner through and through, she loves her peaches and pecans while curling up with a good book. A master of resourcefulness, her love of research leads her down paths of discovery that touch every aspect of her writing. Her love of reading ignited her passion for writing, leading her to frequently fill page after page with tales of her beloved characters' adventures. She loves to sprinkle facts about her beloved Georgia throughout her fictional worlds as an influence and an adversary.

Milton Davis

Milton Davis is a Black Speculative fiction writer and owner of MVmedia, LLC, a small publishing company specializing in Science Fiction, Fantasy and Sword and Soul. MVmedia's mission is to provide speculative fiction books that represent people of color in a positive manner. Milton is the author of seventeen novels; his most recent is the Sword and Soul adventure *Son of Mfumu*. He is the editor and co-editor of seven anthologies; *The City, Dark Universe* with Gene Peterson; *Griots: A Sword and Soul Anthology and Griot: Sisters of the Spear*, with Charles R. Saunders; *The Ki Khanga Anthology*, the *Steamfunk! Anthology*, and the *Dieselfunk anthology* with Balogun Ojetade. MVmedia has also published *Once Upon A Time in Afrika* by Balogun Ojetade and *Abegoni: First Calling* and *Nyumbani Tales* by Sword and Soul creator and icon Charles R. Saunders. Milton's work had also been featured in *Black Power: The Superhero Anthology*; *Skelos2: The Journal of Weird Fiction and Dark Fantasy Volume 2, Steampunk Writes Around the World* published by Luna Press and *Bass Reeves Frontier Marshal Volume Two*.

CPSIA information can be obtained
at www.ICGtesting.com
Printed in the USA
LVHW03s2318150618
580966LV00001B/24/P